# if you're gone

# gone

## BRITTANY GOODWIN

edge of 22
PUBLISHING

Photograph and Cover design by John Goodwin
Interior design by Derek Murphy
Cover model: Tara Thomas

ISBN: 978-0-9975790-0-0

Publisher's Cataloging-in-Publication Data
provided by Five Rainbows Cataloging Services
Names: Goodwin, Brittany.
Title: If you're gone / Brittany Goodwin.
Description: Nashville : Edge of 22, 2016. | Summary: If You're Gone traces a trying summer
    for rising high school senior Lillian White as she struggles to cope with the sudden
    disappearance of her boyfriend.
Identifiers: LCCN 2016907914 | ISBN 978-0-9975790-0-0 (pbk.) | ISBN 978-0-9975790-1-7
    (hardcover)
Subjects: CYAC: Missing persons--Fiction. | High school students--Fiction. | Friendship--
    Fiction. | Secrets--Fiction. | North Carolina--Fiction. | Mystery and detective stories. |
    BISAC: YOUNG ADULT FICTION / Girls & Women. | YOUNG ADULT FICTION /
    Mysteries & Detective Stories. | GSAFD: Mystery fiction. | Suspense fiction.
Classification: LCC PZ7.1.G64 If 2016 (print) | LCC PZ7.1.G64 (ebook) | DDC [Fic]--dc23.

First Edition: June 2016

For the families of the missing. May your loved ones be found and your hearts be healed.

*So we do not lose heart. Though our outer self is wasting away, our inner self is being renewed day by day.* 2 Corinthians 4:16

if you're

gone

*prologue*

I HAD THAT DREAM AGAIN. THE ONE WHERE I'M
back at graduation, wearing an oversized hourglass on a chain
around my neck. Colorful grains of sand rush through it,
representing the remaining time we have together. As the final
grains fall, I am kneeling at my bedroom window, watching
you disappear. Your body fades away as though you are
evaporating into thin air. It's the type of dream I
should probably relay to a shrink, if only I weren't too proud
to admit how losing you has affected every aspect of my life.
Whoever started the rumor that teenagers haven't lived long
enough to understand what true love is didn't know us.

Anyway, what I wanted to say is that I miss you and I think about you every day. I wonder where you are, and what you are doing, and hope you sometimes think of me, too. I try not to regret the decision I made, but often question how different my life might be if I hadn't left you there that day. I ask myself, if I could, would I go back and stop everything from changing? Probably. I would go back for you. You were my world.

# 1

## the best (last) night of my life

HE DIDN'T COME HOME LAST NIGHT.

My heart pounded as I replayed the message a second time. After waking up to my buzzing phone signaling four missed calls and a voicemail marked urgent, I expected to hear juicy gossip from Jason Hamilton's graduation party. Instead, I learned that my boyfriend was nowhere to be found.

"Brad said the two of you had plans after the ceremony, was he headed somewhere after he dropped you off at home? I know it's early, but call me back as soon as you get this."

"He isn't with me," I assured Brad's mom when I returned her calls. "But please let me know when you hear from him."

"I will," Mrs. Lee promised before hanging up. "And you

do the same."

She wasn't as frantic as her message had let on, but there was an unsettling tone in her voice. We both knew it wasn't typical of Brad to stay out all night without telling anyone. *Not anymore, anyway.*

My mind wandered back to the Lions Port High graduation ceremony the night before—squished next to my best friend, Anna Redmond, in the packed football stadium watching Brad accept his diploma. It had been a perfect North Carolina evening; complete with a romantic, lakeside picnic that Brad and I shared once he was able to shed his cap and gown.

I snatched my cell phone off my lap and dialed the number that had lived at the top of my 'favorite contacts' list for the past six months. *Please Lord,* I prayed silently, *let him answer.*

"Hi." I heard the deep voice on the other end and opened my mouth to speak. "You've reached Brad Lee. Leave a message."

His outbound greeting sounded cold and unfriendly, which made me realize I had never gotten his voicemail; he always answered the phone when I called.

"Hey, it's Lillian," I said after the tone, clutching his silver class ring that hung on a chain around my neck. "Your mom has been calling me trying to find you. Is everything all right? Let me know where you are, okay?"

Suddenly, I remembered a detail from the night before and felt a rush of panic. I pictured Brad tapping on my bedroom window and saying those three little words for the first time. *The words* I had been dying to hear. *Does he regret his decision to profess his love to me? Could that explain the radio silence?*

I unlocked the screen of my phone again, this time dialing Anna. My thumb drummed anxiously against the back of the plastic case as it rang.

"Hello?" Anna's usually chipper voice sounded muffled over the line, assumedly lying in her bed with the phone sandwiched between her head and her leopard-print pillow.

"Sorry, were you asleep?"

"It's the first day of summer and it's only nine am," she groaned. "Do I need to remind you how to send a text?"

"I'm sorry," I lied. "But you're the one who sleeps with your cell."

"Yeah, yeah," she spoke clearer this time, although her tone dripped with sarcasm. "I didn't need my beauty sleep anyway."

I scoffed, but I knew she had expected me to laugh. Anna, arguably the most beautiful girl in our junior class, could look runway ready after cramming all night for a test and skipping a shower.

"Are you okay?" she asked.

Anna was a true best friend—she could read my emotions even through a subtle grunt.

"Maybe…" I sighed. "Can you come over?"

"Will there be coffee?"

"I'm sure I can scrounge something up."

"You owe me," she laughed.

"I know. Bye." I pressed end and clutched the warm phone in my hand as I attempted to sort through my thoughts, reliving every detail from the previous night. The ceremony. The picnic. The lake. *The window.*

\*\*\*\*

From my spot on the bleachers I could see the entire senior class, seated in straight rows of plastic folding chairs and dressed in traditional sets of black caps and gowns. Strands of my long, auburn hair danced in the warm May breeze as I sat with my elbows rested on my knees. My attention was split between the football field and my friends beside me.

"That will be us next year, guys!" Anna shouted over the sounds of the stadium. She motioned towards the robed graduates, keeping her fingers interlaced between those of her eight-month serious boyfriend–the tall, dark, and handsome captain of the basketball team, Thomas Grant.

"Only if you don't fail out of AP Chemistry," Thomas said with a laugh.

"Says the jock who signed up for drama and wood shop!" Anna nuzzled her face into his neck before nudging me with her elbow. "Lillian, he's next!"

"I see him!" I exclaimed, staring straight ahead. It was impossible to tear my eyes away from him.

"Bradley Jeremiah Lee." Principal Carver's voice echoed over the loudspeaker.

Brad emerged from the sea of graduates, strutting towards the podium in his cap and gown like a slow motion scene from those nineties teen movies I loved to watch. His tousled blond hair fell into his blue eyes as cheers from the crowd provided a soundtrack for his moment in the spotlight. When he flipped his head to toss the strands back into place his gaze met mine. Even in a packed stadium he could find me.

My face lit up with a giant, ear-to-ear grin as he continued to travel down the aisle, the corners of my mouth practically bursting through the apples of my cheeks. I gave him a small nod and watched him take the first step onto the stage. The crowd around me roared as he accepted his diploma, but I was still. Before Brad, I had never known what it was like to be so captivated by someone that just seeing them glance in your direction could take your breath away. But then, before Brad I had never felt as though I needed someone else just to breathe. There were days I couldn't believe that he was mine—not because of his chiseled jaw and heart-stopping smile, but because he was the most incredible guy I had ever met.

He hadn't always been that way, though. For years, I had avoided him and the group of delinquents he ran around our small town with like the plague. But after a chance encounter six months earlier, I realized that behind his tough exterior was a kind, sincere soul desperate to break away from the friends who were holding him back. And he chose me to help him do that.

"Okay, Lil, you can wipe your drool now. You are literally going to make me throw up. All over you, all over the crowd, everywhere." Anna shook her head and smiled.

"Please don't."

"Then lean in!" She held her cell phone in front of her face and motioned Thomas and me together with one hand. "It's officially summer, kids!" We all squeezed in next to each other, pursing our lips and turning our best angles towards the camera. It was a moment worth capturing.

****

Once the ceremony ended I rushed onto the field with Anna

and Thomas in tow, eager to find Brad amongst the sea of robed seniors.

"Lillian! Anna!" a high-pitched voice called out.

I turned to see Mandy Parton, who insisted she was a distant relative of the big-busted country singer with the same last name, teetering towards us in platform heels. She waved hysterically as her blonde curls bounced against her bare shoulders. Her friend and sidekick Tess Samuels followed, her dark skin looked flawless against her off-white dress.

"Hey guys, there you are!" Tess exclaimed, flipping her raven colored hair behind her shoulder. "Where were you sitting?"

"Front row. Someone wanted a good view," Anna joked, reaching out to hug them.

"They should have had you sing at this shindig, Lil," Mandy said. "Two hours with no music was brutal."

"Maybe next year," I said with a smile. "I got accepted into Honors Choir!"

"Shut up!" Mandy poked my shoulder. "At least someone from this wretched little town might end up famous!"

I laughed as two warm hands reached around my face and covered my eyes. I would have recognized the fresh, light scent of his cologne anywhere.

"I missed you," Brad whispered into my ear.

"Hey!" I spun around and fell into his arms. My cheek pressed up against his collarbone as he wrapped me in his signature bear hug. "I missed you too." It sounded cliché, but I missed him when we were apart, no matter how short the time.

"You are a vision," he said as he reached for my hands,

looking me up and down. "I'm so glad that's over."

"It was great!" I exclaimed. "The best walking I've seen in a while." My toothy grin was growing again.

"Yeah, the dress suits you, too," Thomas snickered, pointing at Brad's shin-length black gown.

"I'll let you try it on later," Brad told him with a smirk as they bumped fists. Just as Brad turned back towards me, a tattooed hand clutched his shoulder.

"Jason's grad party. See you there."

High school drop out Michael Lizardo, appropriately known to his friends and enemies as *Lizard*, appeared behind us, staring at Brad with bloodshot eyes. He was hardly dressed for the occasion in a pair of ripped jeans and a faded black band t-shirt.

"Lizard, don't you actually have to *graduate* to go to a grad party?" Thomas grunted.

"Hey, watch it, pretty boy." Lizard bowed his chest and pulled his elbows back, like a rooster trying to pick a fight. Thomas threw up his hands, laughing as Brad re-positioned himself between them.

"What?" Lizard cocked his head. "You think that's funny?"

"It was a joke, man," Thomas said from behind Brad's shoulder.

Anna and I exchanged a knowing glance. Brad's decision to be with me put him in a constant state of in-between, somewhere between a past life and a future one.

"I'm not coming tonight, all right? We have plans." Brad motioned towards me and I hung on the words 'I'm not coming' instead of 'I can't' since it made it sound like it was all his decision.

"Well, I've got some information you're gonna want," Lizard told him.

"Can it wait?"

Lizard shrugged his shoulders and shot me a hateful glance I hoped he would quickly break, but his eyes lingered. He cocked his head to the side as he stared at me, sending shivers up my spine. "Hope she's worth it."

Brad took another step towards him. "Hey, cut it out…"

"Whatever, man. Don't come crying to me when you get sick of your new Sunday school friends." Lizard turned and offered one last shrewd look at us before he disappeared into the crowd. I realized my heart was racing.

"Always a pleasure, that one," Anna grumbled.

"I'm sorry," Brad said as he wrapped his arms around my waist. "Don't worry about him." He let out a soft sigh but I couldn't read the intention behind it.

"It's okay. Did you want to find your parents?" I changed the subject, willing my pulse to slow, and looked up at him as I gave him a nudge. "I'm sure they want to get photos."

He responded only with a nod.

"We'll be hanging out at Thomas's later if you decide to come by," Anna reminded me.

"Sounds good."

"Bye, guys. Thanks for coming, I mean it."

Brad grabbed my hand and led me behind him through the crowd that had descended upon the football field, my fingers melting in-between his. We weaved in and out of groups of people, every few seconds he would turn to make sure I was still behind him, as though his grip on my hand wasn't enough. *Don't worry. I won't let go. Ever,* I wanted to say. But instead I smiled at him with soft eyes, hoping he already knew.

****

After photo sessions and endless smiles, Brad and I retreated to one of our favorite spots—a secluded, grassy nook in Grissom Park beside a small lake. A crocheted blanket I brought from home lay beneath us as we feasted on the bucket of fried chicken we picked up on the way. The moon lit up the water like a giant spotlight illuminating our picnic.

Brad swallowed a mouthful of chicken and shook a greasy drumstick at me. "Now that school's out and I'm picking up more hours at the hardware store, I'm thinking it's about time I took you out on a nice, fancy date."

I laughed, covering my mouth with my hand in case any meat had found its way in between my teeth. "Oh yeah? Fancy date, huh?"

"Real fancy," he put on a thick southern drawl, much unlike his usual deep timbre. "I mean, I'm talking dinner, movie, and…wait for it…ice cream afterward."

"Wow honey," I mimicked his accent. "That sure is fancy!"

"Hey, just wait." He moved closer on the blanket and lowered his voice, tossing his bare drumstick into the bucket. "I might even wear khakis."

"Yeah, right," I laughed. "I won't count on it."

I wiped my fingers on a napkin and stood up, ambling backward towards the lake as I smiled at him. I didn't have to ask him to follow me; my eyes did the talking and in an instant he was next to me. His arm wrapped around my hip, pulling me close as we continued down to the water. We stopped at the edge of the grass and I leaned against him, feeling his chest rise and fall with each breath as I watched the moonbeams danced across the water. Crickets chirped in the distance. I couldn't remember ever experiencing a moment that was so perfect.

"You saved my life, Lillian," he whispered.

I stared into his eyes; they looked a deeper shade of blue than I had ever seen. "I didn't do anything."

Brad turned his body towards mine, using his hand on my back to pull me into him until we were face to face. Goosebumps raised on my arms as the tip of his nose brushed against my forehead.

"No, Lillian, you have no idea. Without you, I'd be messed up at that crazy graduation party with Lizard. Before you, before *us*, I wasted so much time on things that didn't matter."

I bashfully looked away and gazed out over the water.

"But instead..." he continued. "I'm here. With you. And it's perfect."

I smiled to myself and looked back at him. "It is perfect, isn't it?" Moments with Brad had been perfect since the first kiss we shared, sitting on my living room floor in front of a blazing fire.

Without a word he swept me off the ground, leaving my legs dangling over the lake as he swung his arms, pretending to toss me into the water. "Brad!" I shrieked. "Don't even think about it."

He let out an evil laugh and spun me around, my toes clinging to my jeweled flip-flops. My shrill tones varied from screams to laughter as he carried me across the grass. Aside from Anna, Brad was the only person who could make me laugh until my eyes watered and my sides hurt, struggling to catch my breath between giggles. Our voices echoed across the park, breaking the otherwise serene silence, but it didn't matter. It was perfect.

****

We enjoyed a moonlit wade in the lake, then wrapped the remains of our picnic into the blanket and headed towards my father's car, which he had loaned me for the evening.

"I hope riding around in your dad's sedan isn't ruining you for my truck," Brad said with a smile.

"Nope." I shook my head. "I love your truck."

I handed Brad the keys, and he held the passenger door for me as I climbed inside, slipping a towel onto the bucket seat to protect the leather from my wet skin. We spent most of the drive in silence as I watched the little red numbers change on the LED clock, knowing we would be hard pressed to make my ten o'clock curfew.

"I hope I hear you through the speakers one day," Brad said over the ballad that played softly on the radio. "You're a better singer than half these people."

"Only half, huh?"

"You know what I mean," he said with a grin, reaching across the seat to squeeze my hand. "I'm your biggest fan."

I laced my fingers between his and smiled to myself. "You're sweet."

"Hey, you're going to be late if we go to my house first," he told me, with a nod towards the clock. "I'll take you home and then I can walk from there."

Brad's home was less than a mile from my own, a few blocks up the quiet street where both Anna and I lived, in a newly developed neighborhood stacked with prestigious two-story homes.

"Are you sure? It's so dark out," I said, gazing out the window at the black sky full of twinkling stars.

"You worry about me too much," he laughed and took his eyes off the road for a moment to glance at me.

*That's because I care so much about you,* I wanted to say, although 'care' wasn't a strong enough word. But I held my tongue and grinned at him. I wondered if he knew what I was thinking.

He parked Dad's car in its usual spot, beneath a tall evergreen tree in our driveway. 9:58 pm blinked on the clock as he turned off the humming engine. Brad opened my door for me and we walked hand in hand up the sidewalk to the front door. The house was dark except for the small porch light that had attracted dozens of tiny, white moths. Open fields filled with fireflies enveloped the brick ranch home—our own little piece of paradise, as my mother had referred to it since I was young.

"I had a great time with you tonight," Brad said as we climbed the steps.

"Me too." I ran my fingers up his forearm. "Will you text me and tell me you got home okay?"

He smiled. "My phone's dead. But don't worry. I'll look twice before I cross the street."

"Yeah, yeah." I rolled my eyes.

"I'll call you tomorrow. I'll pick you up at seven for the movies, okay?"

"Sounds great," I said. "I'll even let you decide what we see."

"Don't tease me," Brad said with a laugh, jabbing at my hip bone. We shared a love for movies in every genre, but he always let me have the final say in film selection.

"I mean it! There are several romantic comedies you can choose between."

"You're lucky you're so cute." He grinned. "I'll get the truck cleaned up in the morning. Thanks for the perfect night."

There was that word again. "My pleasure."

He pulled me towards him and we shared a quick goodnight kiss; it was simple with closed lips in case a family member peered through the peephole.

"Lillian?" Brad said as his lips left mine, still holding my face in his hands.

"Yeah?" I whispered. I held my breath, hoping this moment might be the one I had been longing for.

He opened his mouth to speak but then shook his head. "Never mind."

"Are you okay?"

"Never been better." He smiled before planting a wet smack on my cheek. "Good night."

I slipped my key into the lock and waved to him as he descended the steps.

"Good night!" I called out, grinning. I realized it didn't matter he hadn't said the words. They were written all over his face.

Inside the entryway, I eased the door shut behind me, using care to click the latch quietly into place. To my right was the living room, where I had expected to see my parents; Mom's face in a book nestled under the reading lamp, worn out from a long day on her feet at the department store where she worked, while Dad came in and out of sleep in front of the television, still dressed in his business shirt and tie. But, like the foyer, it was dark. It seemed that Brad's graduation night came with a special privilege—not being nagged about what we did and where we ate and who was there. The usual grilling.

I felt my way down the hall to my bedroom, letting my fingers drag the chair rail as I took long, light-footed strides. I passed the closed doors that led into my little brother and sister's rooms. Silence. Ages ten and eight, Graham and Eliza had likely been asleep for hours. Light from the television danced under my parents' door but there were no sounds of movement inside. It was eerily quiet, a rare instance in the White household.

Behind my bedroom door, I took a deep breath as I retrieved the oversized t-shirt that Brad had given me weeks ago. Even though I had worn it every night it still smelled like him—spicy with a hint of citrus. His ring felt cool against my chest as I changed.

I turned off the light and rushed across the cool wood floor, pulling the chain on my bedside lamp as I scurried under the comforter. Once I was nestled beneath the covers I reached for the paperback novel on my nightstand and flipped it open to a dog-eared page, but it was impossible to focus on the words in front of me. I didn't need to read a fictional boy-meets-girl story when Brad's goodbye kiss was lingering on my lips. I closed my eyes and tried to imagine him next to me, but just as I began to picture his blue eyes a tree branch snapped outside my window.

The little hairs on my arm stood up as I remembered the odd silence in the house, the dark rooms showing no signs of life. *Crack.* There it was again. My toes curled under the covers. I returned the book to my nightstand and waited, holding my breath as I listened. My oversized window faced the backside of an overgrown pine tree in the front of our house. For the past several years my Dad had planned to hire professionals to trim the monstrous tree, but for now it remained a thick, bushy giant that towered above my bedroom in our one story home. I usually didn't mind, it still let in light between its branches and made a nice curtain. But tonight the limbs of the tree seemed to reach around my room like thick fingers in the darkness.

*Crack.* Another sound from outside pierced through the silence, interrupting my thoughts.

"Lillian?" A muffled voice called out my name.

Had I imagined it? I tossed the blanket from my legs, gnawing on my lower lip as I moved towards the window. Grabbing the bottom of the sill, I gritted my teeth as I thrust upwards to open the pane. A cool breeze hit my face and I backed away, squinting while I peered into the darkness. The sound of the crickets filled my room and echoed off the classic movie posters on the walls.

"Lillian?" The voice was clearer this time.

"Hello?" My eyes darted between the tree branches.

"Boo!" Brad exclaimed as he jumped from the ground.

I let out a shrill squeal.

"Shh! Someone will hear you," he whispered, placing a finger against his lips.

"You scared me to death," I said, an unavoidable smile growing on my face. "What are you doing back here?"

"I'm sorry. I need to tell you something. It's important." He leaned in towards the window and reached for my hand as I knelt on the floor to be on his level.

"Brad, what is it?"

"You don't have to say anything." His blue eyes caught the light from my bedroom, shining like piercing stars in the darkness. "But I need you to know."

My chest became heavy as if all of my breath was leaving my body. This was it. The moment I had been hoping for since his lips first met mine six months earlier.

"Lillian…I love you."

The declaration hung in the evening air like lyrics to a beautiful song. I could never have imagined that hearing the words coming from his mouth would sound so natural, so right.

"I love you," he said again, this time less nervous but just as sincere. "So much. Good night!"

As he turned away I realized I hadn't answered him. I had been too busy staring into his eyes.

"Brad! Wait!" I shouted in a voice only slightly louder than a whisper. He rushed back to the window as the words flew off my tongue. "I love you, too!"

We leaned toward each other and our lips met. Somehow, the kiss was different from the hundreds we had shared before.

It was more official. More permanent. When we broke apart he stroked my cheeks with his hands, holding my face close to his.

"I'll see you soon, Lil. I love you."

"I love you too," I echoed. "Good night."

Brad pulled away from our embrace and smiled, offering a quick wink before turning to leave. Sitting on my knees and hugging the window frame, I watched as he disappeared into the darkness. *He was gone.*

# 2

## the first forty-eight

I MET ANNA IN THE DRIVEWAY, HOLDING TWO ceramic mugs brimming with fresh coffee and motioned her to the back deck. She looked glamorous as always, even in an oversized tank top and cut-offs, like a movie star caught by the lens of paparazzi.

"So, how was your date?" Anna asked with a wide yawn as she accepted the coffee from my outstretched hand. She nestled into the green paisley cushion draped across a wrought-iron bench on the deck. A handful of small birds fluttered overhead, darting at each other as they passed.

"It was great. Really great..." I sighed, letting my body melt into the chair beside her as I fiddled with the ring around my neck.

"Oh my gosh, don't tell me. Did you…" Her eyes grew wide.

"Shh! No!" I glanced back towards the kitchen window to make sure Graham and Eliza weren't eavesdropping through the screen. "But he told me he loved me."

Anna nearly dropped her coffee onto the side table, quickly swallowing the hot liquid that remained in her mouth.

"Shut up! What did you say? Do you tell him you love him?"

I smiled as I nodded. "Yes! I just said 'I love you too'. It was kind of magical."

"I mean, I knew you were crushing hard, but love? No wonder you woke me up at the butt-crack of dawn. I've been trying to get Thomas to drop the L-bomb for like months. Even though I'm pretty sure the guys on the basketball team are trying to convince him he's whipped," she laughed. "I'm so sorry for doubting that you had huge news!" Anna reached for her coffee, her face frozen in a bewildered grin.

I glanced at my hands as I wrung them in my lap, my smile fading. "That's not really what I called you for, though."

"Don't tell me, did you get engaged, too?" she asked with a giggle.

"No. Nothing like that."

"Okay, okay." She cleared her throat. "I'm sorry. Go ahead."

"Mrs. Lee called and told me Brad didn't come home last night," I told her. "She doesn't know where he is."

"And he wasn't with you?"

I shook my head.

"Well, where could he be?"

I let my head fall back into the chair as I let out a groan. "I have no idea. That's the whole problem. I've called him like twenty times."

"Maybe he went to Jason's party and just ended up crashing there." Anna sipped her coffee, pursing her lips as she swallowed.

"Anything is possible, I suppose," I agreed. "But Brad never goes to parties anymore. Let alone crash somewhere. It doesn't sound like something he'd do."

"You're right." Anna took a deep breath. "But, just thinking out loud...is there a chance that he had planned to go out and didn't tell you?" She turned her head away from me as she spoke and stared out into the yard.

"No, why would he do that?" I asked defensively.

"I'm just saying, Lillian," she said with a shrug. "It's not like you and Lizard are exactly friends, so maybe Brad wanted to go to the party with him but didn't want you to be upset."

"Trust me, Brad doesn't want to go anywhere with Lizard."

"Okay, so maybe he just wanted to go, but he knew you couldn't because of your curfew."

"No." I shook my head. "He would have told me."

"Well, does he tell you everything?"

*He tells me he loves me.*

"Look, I wouldn't worry about it too much," she continued on in a nonchalant voice. "In this town, you can't get far without someone seeing you. I'm sure he's around and he has a perfectly good explanation."

"You're right," I said, nodding as I remembered a detail from the night. "We're going to the drive-in tonight at seven! Although I hope I won't have to wait that long for answers…"

A grin spread across Anna's face and she let out a laugh.

"What is so funny?"

She continued to smile. "You do love him."

"Yes!" I exclaimed. "What, you didn't believe me before?"

****

Anna left to go bathing suit shopping with her mom and I hung on her words to 'not worry' for about thirty seconds. *Of course I'm going to worry.* My fingers dialed Brad's number again and I listened to the single ring before the call was sent to voicemail. I couldn't decide if I should be more concerned that he didn't seem to be contacting anyone, or that he hadn't contacted *me*.

"Brad, it's me again. Please call me," I said after the beep. "Your parents are worried about you and so am I." I lowered the phone to end the call before jerking it back towards my mouth. "I love you."

I tried not to panic. My mind raced with scenarios that kept Brad from both going home or returning calls, some positive, but mostly negative. I called and texted everyone I could think of who might know where to find him, but the answers were all the same. No one claimed to have seen him since the graduation ceremony. All I wanted was for the phone to buzz and to hear Brad's voice on the other line, with a logical explanation for his disappearance

I re-dialed Brad's home number and Mrs. Lee and I spoke

at length about where he might be and what we should do. She said Brad's truck was still parked in their driveway and showed no signs of being moved since before the graduation ceremony, but we agreed it wasn't unusual for him to make his way around our sleepy town on foot. She informed me Brad's dad had called the hospital, the jail, and finally the police, all to no avail. Mr. Lee talked to a detective who encouraged them to be patient and wait for him to come home on his own.

"Some kids have a little too much fun on graduation night," he told him.

We ended our conversation on the promise that we would call each other as soon as we heard from Brad, holding on to the hope he would arrive for our seven o'clock date as planned. I assured her that I'd continue to reach out to our classmates, and she promised to do the same. But there was one phone number I didn't have, and it was for the one person I had to speak with.

I drove my mom's SUV into town, scanning every sidewalk and storefront for a glimpse of Brad as I passed until I came upon the weathered community bulletin board on High Street. Lost dog posters and advertisements for babysitters were tacked and taped onto the wooden board. Stuck in the center I saw a faded car repair ad scrawled in black permanent marker, right where I expected to find it.

*Lizard's Car Repair. Call anytime.*

I punched the number into my cell phone and returned to the SUV as I hit send. *One ring. Two rings.* Just as the third ring began it was suddenly interrupted by an automated voicemail message.

"The person you are trying to reach has a voice mailbox that has not been set up yet."

"So that's how you're going to play this, huh?" I said to myself, swiping the screen to end the call. I stared at the phone for a moment before opening a text message.

*I'm looking for Brad, can you tell me where he is?* I typed. *Send.*

Within moments, a new message appeared.

*Who wants 2know*

I gasped. *This is Lillian. I need to find Brad ASAP. Please just answer me.*

I sent the message and waited anxiously, but after several minutes I had still not received a response.

*Please, Lizard. Do you know where he is?*

I waited again. Finally, my phone buzzed. I held my breath as I read the message.

*No. Why would I. How did U get this #*

I began typing another reply but stopped myself. What else was there to say? I let out a heavy sigh and ran my fingers through my unwashed hair. I knew it was the answer I had wanted, but now I was right back where I started. I turned the car key and sat in neutral, staring blankly at the handful of pedestrians that passed by on the sidewalk. *He didn't go to a party. He isn't with Lizard. He isn't with me. And he isn't at home. Brad, where are you?* As I pulled away from the curb, I prayed silently. *Dear Lord, please let Brad be okay. Let us be okay.*

\*\*\*\*

I drove around town for over an hour, checking in at the retro diner we loved, the hardware store where Brad worked, and several convenience stores where he often purchased a canned energy drink and a stick of beef jerky for an afternoon pick-me-up. I jumped every time my phone vibrated. He didn't call. The Lees had insisted I call them by 7:15 pm if he didn't show up for our date. I pictured them seated in their living room, eyes locked on the front door and one hand on the telephone.

In an attempt to shove all worries aside, I dressed for the evening, in a flowing pastel halter-top over dark-rinse jeans. I pinned my hair half back, letting my natural wave add volume to my otherwise mousy tresses. I applied an extra coat of mascara and dusted highlighting powder across my cheekbones, hoping to achieve a rested, youthful look even after a day of stress. But as I paced in front of the living room window, squeezing his class ring and praying for his truck to pull into my driveway, it was clear I was wasting precious time. He wasn't coming. As the clock changed to 7:02 pm, any remaining hope was shattered. Brad was never late. I had been stood up. And something was very wrong.

Mrs. Lee picked up on the first ring and sputtered an anxious "Hello!" into the phone.

"He isn't here." My throat tightened, choking on the words.

"Thank you, Lillian. We are calling the police again now." She hung up without a goodbye. We both knew there was nothing that could be said.

****

The rest of the night felt like a foggy dream. The Lees and I organized an impromptu search party and within the hour dozens of my classmates and members of the community gathered on my front lawn, equipped with flashlights and rain ponchos as a dreary drizzle fell from the summer sky. My dad printed off hundreds of posters at his real estate office and Mr. Lee handed them out in stacks under our carport, spouting off instructions to hang them on every storefront and telephone pole. A group of searchers split up at the edge of my yard, dragging their feet and crouching low, shining their lights through the grass as they headed down the street. It was as though they expected to find Brad in tiny pieces, scattered along the roadway.

I made my way through the crowds of people on my lawn the same way I had at the graduation ceremony, only without Brad's hand to guide me. *He would never just leave me alone like this.* A handful of passing classmates stopped to offer their condolences, an opportunity I took to further beg for information. But just as they had on the phone, none of the members of Brad's graduating class claimed to have seen him at any parties the night before, which I found to be both disappointing and reassuring. *It has to be true. He wouldn't have lied to me. But if he didn't lie to me, where is he?*

Planting myself near the sidewalk, I took an inventory of the crowd. There were more people than I could count, mostly familiar faces from school and church, but some strangers. A brunette boy I didn't recognize caught my eye and gave me a nod, which I returned before dropping my eyes to the ground. The tips of my ears burned, making me wonder if people were talking about me.

I scanned the yard for my friends and found Tess and Mandy standing in the driveway speaking with Mrs. Lee. I had interrupted Anna and Thomas's date with a phone call informing them that Brad was still missing and there would be a search. They were due to arrive within the hour. Amongst the groups of people on my lawn, there was no sign of law enforcement and almost more notably, no sign of Lizard.

I unlocked my phone and scrolled through dozens of numbers in my recent outgoing call list until I came to his, quickly tapping send before I could change my mind.

After two rings the electronic voice greeted me with the same message I had received earlier in the day. "The person you've called has a voice mailbox that has not been set up yet."

I hung up and touched send again. "Come on, just pick up."

"Stop calling me," a gruff male voice came on the line.

"Lizard?" *Silence.* "Lizard, wait!" I shouted before he hung up. "Everyone is looking for Brad. I need you to tell me if you've seen him or know where he might be."

"I already told you I ain't seen him."

"Well, you could at least come over here and help us look for him. We're all worried…"

"And why would I do that?" he snapped. "Sounds like you can't keep tabs on your man." He let out a deep, cackling laugh.

"This isn't a joke, Michael." I gritted my teeth, knowing he hated being called by his first name. "Brad's missing. There's a search party gathering on my front lawn…"

"I'm tellin' you one last time, I have no idea where he is."

"I swear," I said. "If you know something you aren't telling me…"

"The only thing I've got to tell you is *stop calling me*. And you can tell Brad's mommy and daddy to stop bugging me, too. This is harassment."

There was a click on the line. He was gone. Disregarding his demand, I sent the call again, but the phone went directly to the recorded message. I let out a tortured groan as I turned to see Anna rushing towards me with outstretched arms.

"Lillian, are you okay?" She pulled me in for a hug and squeezed my shoulders. All I could do was shrug. "Let's go find Brad. Come on, I'll drive."

\*\*\*\*

A group of us piled into Anna's blue compact car and rode in silence to the outskirts of downtown, where we planned to plaster posters on storefronts and search the alleys for any signs of Brad. I leaned my head against the passenger window as Anna drove; my eyes darted around the buildings we passed. Our usually peaceful little town seemed darker and quieter than ever, as if it were keeping a secret. I pictured Lions Port pulling Brad into the atmosphere and trapping him in another dimension from where he was watching us look for him, screaming my name to get my attention. This alternate reality theory was preferable to the actuality of what was happening.

As the car crept along a side street my gaze fell to a thin alleyway, sandwiched between Meyer's Deli and an empty building that once housed a children's dance studio where Anna and I had taken ballet. The moonlight bounced off of the tall brick walls, casting giant shadows in the alley as long streaks of rain glimmered under the streetlights. In the darkness, I saw movement and my heart dropped from my chest.

"Stop the car! Stop!" I shouted as I frantically fiddled with my seatbelt, feeling trapped beneath the straps.

Anna jerked the wheel and pulled to a stop before she had a chance to speak.

"It's him. I saw him." It took all of my breath to spit out the words.

Trembling, I pushed my weight against the door and had my feet on the pavement as Anna threw down the gearshift to put the car in park. I darted across the sidewalk and into the dark alleyway, moving as fast as I could yet feeling like I was dragging my body through quicksand. My heart was racing and my hands were shaking as I stumbled into the shadowy alley. I began anxiously searching the spaces behind empty dumpsters and abandoned pallets.

"Brad!" I cried out, my voice cracking as I yelled. His name echoed into the night. "Brad? Are you there?"

Frozen in place, I held my breath and prayed a frantic prayer. *Please let him be here. Please Lord, let me hear him. Please let me see him.*

But there was no response from Brad, no sign of life, not even an alley cat. I was alone.

"Brad," I sputtered, clutching his ring. "Where are you?"

I placed my hands on my knees as I caught my breath, letting my head hang. The cool rain dropped against my back while I panted. I heard footsteps rushing towards me and looked up, peering through ragged strands of hair that had fallen across my face. Anna and Thomas, followed by Mandy and Tess who were huddled together under a polka dot umbrella, stared at me with wide eyes as they approached.

"Lillian, are you okay?" Anna clutched my shoulder, crouching to meet my eyes. "What did you see?"

*I imagined him.*

"It was nothing," I whispered. I tried to stand tall, but I suddenly felt as though bricks were tied to my chest. A dull ache took over my entire body, beginning at the top of my skull and working its way to the tips of my pink toenails. My eyelids were heavy; I was exhausted. My face was wet but I couldn't tell if it was from the rain or if I was crying.

"I'm so sorry," Anna shook her head as she spoke. She wrapped her arms around me in a hug and my knees went weak as I melted into her grasp.

I felt Thomas's arm come across my back as Tess held the umbrella over us. We stood there for several minutes, huddled together in the dark alleyway. When our group released the embrace, I straightened up and watched as a poster slipped from the stack in Anna's hand and fell into a small puddle at my feet. I kept my eyes fixed on Brad's face as the ink dissolved into the water, his silhouette disappearing from the paper. The bricks in my chest were weighing me down again. I wanted to collapse onto the ground. Even on paper, he was gone.

# 3

## a kiss can change your world

ANNA HELD MY HAND AS I SAUNTERED BACK TO
her car. With every step the atmosphere seemed to grow colder
and thinner; I could smell the chill in the air. Thomas opened
the passenger door and Anna helped me into the bucket seat.
My knees were shaking as I sank into the cushions.

"We should hang these posters up before we head back. Is
that okay with you?" Anna spoke slowly and softly, as though I
were a fragile child.

"Of course that's okay."

"One of us should stay here with her," Tess told
them under her breath.

"I'm fine." I shook my head. "I want to be alone."

"Okay, Lil, we will be right outside the car if you need us. Lock the doors."

Anna pushed the passenger door shut and stepped up onto the sidewalk with the others. She started handing out small stacks of Brad's posters to the group but I had to turn away. I couldn't watch them plaster his face all over our town like he was some kind of wanted felon. I held back tears as I wrapped my arms around myself, overcome with a chill from the night air. The cold reminded me of Brad. It reminded me of love and how my life had changed forever on an unsuspecting snowy day, six months before. As I nestled into the seat, I closed my eyes and remembered that day like it was a movie playing out in my head.

****

It was late November, and the snow from the night before lay thick on the grass and road in front of me. A snow day with Anna had come to an end, and I headed home as her mother and stepfather sat down for dinner. We knew school would inevitably be canceled the following day, for the sky had opened up again and quarter-size flakes were falling. I was bundled in my thick brown winter jacket and topped off with a purple and blue striped scarf and hat set my grandmother had knitted for me a few winters back. I fiddled around in my jacket pocket for my gloves, but could only recover one.

Nestling my left hand deep into my coat, I picked up my pace as I trudged down the street. My breath wasn't visible in the crisp air; the snowfall was too thick. Flakes clung to my eyelashes, and I batted my eyes to see through the falling white. My socks were wet inside my boots from traipsing through the dense snow, and my toes were tingling. When I saw my house in the distance I broke into a sprint across my front lawn. I was only a few paces from the front porch when my foot caught a snow-covered root, sending my body crashing to the ground. I let out a cry that was muffled by my face hitting a hard bank of snow.

I held still, partially frozen and partially stunned. Spitting snow from my mouth, I tried to stand, but my right ankle sent sharp pains up my leg. I lowered myself back down and held in tears I was sure would freeze the moment they left their sockets. With a look to the dark, empty house I knew I'd receive no help from my parents. They had taken Graham and Eliza on a weekend trip and weren't able to return home in the storm. I reached into the pocket of my snow pants for my key, but it was empty. Panicking, I felt around in the powder where I sat, knowing the key must have slipped out when I fell. A warm tear slid down my face as the snow fell harder and a gust of wind whipped the flakes across my skin.

Suddenly, I heard a *crunch* behind me and craned my neck to see a dark figure tramping through the yard in my direction.

"Hello!" I cried out, both frightened and relieved.

"Lillian?" a deep voice said, sending a shiver down my back.

Before I could say anything, a hand firmly grasped my arm. I grew frightened and tried to pull away as I imagined whom the voice might belong to. I tried to peer through the falling snow at the person beside me, but snowflakes blew into my eyes. I raised my gloved hand and brushed the wet hair away from my face. When I recognized the figure that stood in front of me, I gasped.

It was Brad, my middle school tormentor. His dirty blond locks fell in his eyes, glittered with flakes of snow. My throat dropped into my stomach and despite the cold, my face suddenly felt warm.

"I saw you fall, what hurts?" he asked, his piercing blue eyes staring into mine.

"I'm fine, I don't need any help." I kept my gaze locked with his, desperate to appear strong. I attempted to pull away from his grasp, remembering how he had treated me when we were younger. He laughed.

"Lillian, you're obviously hurt. Just let me help you inside."

He was persistent, and I was surprised by the kindness in his voice but didn't want to give in. I thought back to when I had first met Brad. I was in fifth grade and my parents encouraged me to become friends with him when his family moved in down the street. He was cute and seemed more mature than other guys my age, so I didn't argue. But much to my dismay, he denied my friendship and instead bullied and terrorized me on the playground, in the lunchroom, and in the hallways of the school. When I expressed my anger to my mother she had laughed, telling me he must have a crush on me. But before that theory was ever proven, Brad had lost interest in torturing me and moved on to harassing the entire neighborhood with his delinquent group of friends.

Once we entered high school he had become what most girls considered a total hottie, with broad, muscular shoulders and a chiseled jaw that was accentuated by his long, tousled blond hair. But there was always a look in his deep, blue eyes I didn't understand. Although we didn't speak, I would catch him staring at me sometimes and always wondered if he was contemplating apologizing for making my middle school years a nightmare. To this day, no such apology had been made.

"Lillian, come on." His voice interrupted my thoughts. "It's freezing."

"Just help me find my key, I dropped it," I replied, shooting him the coldest look I could muster. I patted the snow around where I fell.

"Lil, it's gone. You won't find that key until spring. I can get you in. Come on." He wrapped one arm around my back and held the other on my hand. I looked into his eyes with intentions to resist, but I let myself give in. His embrace was unfamiliar, yet something told me to trust him.

"Fine, thanks," I mumbled, breaking away from his gaze.

He lifted me from the snowy ground and helped me hobble to the house and up the three front porch steps. He propped me up against the brick wall as he dug through his pockets.

"You okay?" He pulled a plastic card from his back pocket as he spoke.

"I'm fine." I leaned against the cold brick, keeping my ankle elevated.

"All right. Wait here."

Brad fled down the steps, rushing through the banks of snow, and disappeared from view. I listened as I waited, considering that he may have brought me this far and ditched me. But suddenly the front door swung open and snow spilled onto the hardwood floors in the entryway.

"Home at last!" Brad said with a smile, standing in the doorway. He motioned me inside and placed his arm around my waist for support as I took the step up into the foyer. He pressed the door closed against the wind and helped me into the house.

"How did you get in?" I asked as I pointed towards the living room and let him help me to the couch.

He sat me in the corner seat against a pillow before removing his jacket where he stood. "The back door was open."

I shook my head. "Liar."

"Okay, okay. You're right," he said as he knelt in front of me. He untied the boot on my sprained ankle as he spoke. "I'm sorry."

*An apology!* I listened as he continued, wincing in pain when he pulled the shoe from my swollen foot.

"There's always a loose window or a worn out lock."

I raised my eyebrows. "So you've progressed from playground bully to common criminal?"

"Yeah, well, I wouldn't go that far," he told me, grinning. "I know we did some pretty dumb stuff when we were kids. Me and Lizard and Jones…we broke into a few houses." Before I could interrupt he continued. "But we never hurt anybody, and we never stole anything…well, not anything valuable. We would just throw little parties and eat people's food if we knew they were out of town. Stuff like that. It's stupid, I know. And it was a long time ago."

"Well, that's interesting," I replied with a sly grin, watching as he fiddled with my second boot.

"Wasn't it just last month that the Grant's came home from vacation to find an empty fridge and a trashed kitchen?"

Brad looked up at me, surprised. "You sure find it impossible to trust me, don't you?" He didn't wait for me to answer. "And yes, it happened. But Thomas Grant is a pompous jock anyway, so he deserved it." My mouth dropped. "I'm kidding, Lil. I wasn't there. Lizard and Jones still do their thing, but I don't hang around them that much anymore. Since Lizard dropped out of school I really only see him if I'm working on my truck at his shop. Things have changed, you know."

"Yeah," I said with a nod. "Things have changed." I didn't know what else to say. I realized I wanted to believe him, but that meant tearing down the walls between us I had spent over five years building up.

"You don't have to believe me," Brad told me, as if he had read my mind. "I'll prove it to you. Maybe not today or tomorrow, but I will. You'll see."

"So now what?" I asked, shrugging my shoulders. My walls started to crumble as I gave in to the smile that had been creeping up the sides of my mouth. After all, it wasn't every day I was alone in my living room with the hottest guy in school—whether I agreed with that declaration or not.

"Well…I'm looking for something new to occupy my time." His eyes met mine and he smiled. "Something…or someone…to keep me out of trouble."

He held my gaze and my heart started to race faster and faster for every moment I didn't look away. I didn't know how I should feel. All I knew was that I felt something.

**** 

Brad nursed my swollen ankle and wrapped it in a towel bathed in ice as I rested atop a bed of pillows in front of the wood-burning fireplace he had effortlessly lit. He disappeared into the kitchen and I laughed at the thought of him raiding our neighbors' refrigerators. Leaning back onto the leg of the couch, I stared into the glowing flames and became lost in my own thoughts. I compared sixth grade Brad to the guy he was now. The only similar feature was his blue eyes. I had once seen them as cold. But in that moment, the look in his eyes I could never understand suddenly seemed like it was meant for me.

He returned from the kitchen carrying two steaming mugs of hot chocolate. A dozen mini marshmallows floated across the top of the cocoa as he handed it to me.

"No marshmallows for you?" I asked.

"Nah, I'm watching my figure," he replied without so much as a grin as he sat down beside me.

"This is perfect, Brad. Thank you." *Even from day one, it was perfect.*

"You're just lucky your parents keep the cabinets stocked." We laughed. "How are you doing?"

"I'm fine. Maybe my ankle is just frozen from the ice wrap, but it doesn't hurt anymore!" I smiled at him. "I was actually just remembering middle school..."

He groaned. "Man, I've tried to block those years out. I was hoping everyone else had done the same. I was such a jerk!"

"You tormented me," I said with a nod. "Every day. I used to lie awake at night thinking up excuses not to go to school the next day!"

Brad put his hands over his eyes, shaking his head as he groaned. "I wish I could kill whoever taught me to 'snap' a girls' bra strap."

"Yes! I should've reported you for harassment."

"Guilty as charged." Brad held his wrists out in front of him, offering to be handcuffed. "Have them take me away."

"I'm being serious!" I said with a giggle.

"So am I."

I slipped a hair tie off my wrist and positioned it in the middle of his back. "Let the punishment fit the crime." With a sharp *pop*, I snapped the elastic against his spine and he let out a little yelp.

"Hey! Is that what it feels like?"

I shrugged. "Close enough."

"You know, there's something I've been meaning to tell you," he said after a moment.

"Oh yeah?"

"I saw you sing at church a few weeks ago. In the Sunday night service."

"You did?" I asked. "I don't remember seeing you there."

"I was. And you were incredible."

"Incredible?" I grinned. "That's a pretty big word."

"Not big enough," he said, taking my breath away as his gaze met mine.

We laughed and reminisced for what seemed like hours. When the fire grew dim we inched nearer to each other, trying to keep warm as the wind whipped outside the window. Every time our eyes met it felt as though it was impossible for them to be torn away. There was something about him I couldn't believe I hadn't noticed before.

Before I knew it, our eyes were locked, my heart was racing, and I was short of breath. He leaned towards me and I could see the orange glow of the flames flickering in his baby blue eyes as they closed. His lips met mine so suddenly that I felt paralyzed. I closed my eyes tight and let it all soak in. I was kissing Brad Lee.

# 4

## on the permanent record

I WAS AWAKE WHEN THE SUN CREPT THROUGH the window and onto the foot of my wrought iron bed. I lay still for a moment, staring into the light that illuminated the blanket covering my toes. *Deep breath in, deep breath out.* It had now been twenty-four hours since Brad was discovered missing. Particles of dust swam through the stream of light and I considered counting them, hoping it might take long enough and Brad would be found before I even got out of bed. *Deep breath in.* Twisting my body towards the bedside table, I leaned forward to check the clock. 6:24 am. *Deep breath out.* I tried to count the hours of sleep I had gotten that night, but couldn't. All I could remember was lying awake trying not to dream.

From where I lay in my bed, I saw frozen faces sta
at me. Taped to the mirror above my chest of dra
faded photographs from the past three years of high schoo,
with a scattered few of Anna and me in middle school-
capturing my glimmering braces and greasy hair. I had once
spent hours printing my favorite pictures off of my social
media pages, but now I snarled at the smiling faces. *What could
any of us have possibly been so happy about?*

The photo of me and Brad at my junior prom was
displayed in the center with heart stickers as adhesive. My
waved hair was combed to one side and pinned back with a
silver linen flower. The purple dress I wore that night hugged
my body, accentuating my tall, thin frame and had made me
feel more beautiful than ever. And then there was Brad; his
blue eyes the most prominent feature of the picture. From the
bottom of his black tuxedo to the tips of his shaggy blond hair,
he was flawless.

I understood why they chose the photo for his Have You
Seen This Man poster; it captured the essence of Brad
perfectly. But what people didn't see when they looked at that
poster was that that essence was captured when he was
standing next to *me*. A single snip of the scissors had cut me
out of that photo, just like a single moment had somehow cut
Brad out of my life; out of everyone's lives.

My mind wandered back to the night before when we had
returned from hanging posters to find Brad's parents at odds
with a uniformed officer on my front lawn. The search parties
came back empty handed, thousands of posters had been given
out and plastered all over the town, and we were no closer to

finding Brad. I sat on the front porch and listened to the man, later identified as Detective Padron, as he stood under the lamppost in our driveway and explained his take on the situation to Mr. and Mrs. Lee.

It was hard to make out every word he had said, but the general gist of the conversation was quite clear. Brad was eighteen, which meant he was legally considered an adult and had every right to disappear if he wanted to. There were no signs of foul play so the police department wasn't very inclined to offer much energy towards the case. The detective would put out a BOLO (meaning 'be on the lookout' I learned when I immediately looked it up) and question Brad's friends and classmates as necessary, but they wouldn't be calling the FBI or Nancy Grace.

*Give it a few days, chances are he will just come back on his own.* These had been Detective Padron's parting words as he climbed into his squad car. He backed out of our driveway with the blue lights atop his car illuminated but the siren remained off. *No emergency here*, he must have been saying to himself as he drove into the night. Brad, who meant the world to me, our friends, and his family, seemed to be nothing more than an inconvenience to Detective Padron. Still, Mrs. Lee promised that she had insisted he talk with me the following day and he would be returning to my house to do so. I had to wonder, though, if he was coming to question me as Brad's girlfriend, or as the last known person to have seen him.

Glancing back to the clock I grimaced, 6:36 am. I felt as though no amount of sleep would energize me. I wished I could fall into a coma, with a note pinned to my chest that read—*Do not wake unless you are Brad Lee.*

Up until now, I had always found humor in the fact that Brad's parents had given him a first name that, when coinciding with his last name, sounded like one word. *Brad Lee? Or is it Bradley?* I had heard teachers call for him, questionably. But it didn't seem funny anymore; it felt ominous. *That first-name last-name guy is missing.* That might have been all he was to some people, Detective Padron being one of them, but he was so much more to me.

I pinched my eyes closed and attempted to pray, something I had tried several times in over the last two days without success. *Please keep him safe. Please bring him home. Please help me understand this. Please give me strength. Why did you let this happen? Please, please, please.* There it was again. Every attempt at prayer started with pleading and turned into anger. *This isn't fair. What did I do to deserve this? Please just let him be okay. Please don't make me suffer through this for another day.* Prayer wasn't supposed to sound so much like lyrics to a country song.

I started to force myself out of bed when I instead reached for my phone and dialed Brad's number for the umpteenth time. It only rang once. My heart skipped a beat as a woman's voice came on the line.

"I'm sorry, the mailbox is full and cannot accept any messages at this time," a computerized voice informed me before ending the call.

I couldn't see him, I couldn't touch him, I couldn't speak to him, and now I couldn't even hear his voice. *Is there anything left to take from me?*

I wondered who had contributed to filling up his voicemail.

On an average day, his call log would have only shown ingoing and outgoing conversations with me, a message thread with Thomas containing sarcastic remarks and sports scores, and the occasional text from Mrs. Lee about what time dinner would be ready. Now, in his absence, was the whole town attempting to show compassion? I was so sick of questions. *Please, Lord, give me some answers.*

****

I dozed in and out until Eliza tapped me on the shoulder; her tiny frame was barely tall enough to see over the bed.

"Mom says you need to get ready for church." Her slight lisp made the corners of my mouth turn up in my first attempt at a smile since the previous morning.

"Okay. Tell her I'm up."

She nodded and rushed out of the room, likely under instructions not to bother me. As I kicked off the blanket and placed my feet on the rug, my eyes caught the window where I had watched Brad disappear into the night. *He literally disappeared in front of me.* I stood up and ambled across the floor to the window as I had that night. There was a small smudge on the pane I hadn't noticed before. I reached up to wipe it from the glass, only to realize it was on the outside. It might have been a splatter of guts from a suicidal bug or pollen dried in a raindrop from the dreary night before, or it could have been from him. *Maybe a smudged fingerprint is all I have left of our last moments together.* That thought made it too painful to look at.

****

Later that morning I sat beside my parents in our small sanctuary with Anna and her family in the row behind us. I felt like I was attending a funeral, maybe even my own. I was supposed to be on stage with the choir, but instead I was huddled in the fifth row, wanting to disappear into the cushioned pew.

It had been a struggle just to dress myself, as black seemed too hopeless but a summer dress was much too carefree. I was definitely not feeling carefree. The ankle jeans and green V-neck t-shirt I had settled on weren't making much of a statement, but I didn't care.

In the front row sat Mr. and Mrs. Lee, with Brad's ten-year-old sister, Montana, between them. Montana smiled and waved to me with the tips of her fingers. I wondered if she could even comprehend what was happening. Her parents stared straight ahead, still enough to be statues. I didn't understand why we were all sitting around instead of beginning another search. It felt as though everyone had given up on finding Brad after just one night.

"As we close, I'd like us to take a moment to pray for one of our young members, Brad Lee," Pastor Allen spoke from behind the pulpit. "For reasons we do not yet know, he has not contacted his friends or family since Friday evening. If anyone comes in contact with Brad, please urge him to reach out to his family. We pray that this young man is not in any danger and that he will make smart decisions…"

He kept talking, but I didn't want to listen. It was becoming bigger than posters, bigger than un-organized search parties wandering through the ditch in my front yard, bigger than a pre-occupied Detective Padron offering less-than-encouraging words. Our pastor was standing in front of the entire congregation and asking for their help. The members of our church who didn't even recognize Brad when he passed them in the sanctuary would now know him as the Missing Guy. *The first-name last-name missing guy.* What would be next? Assemblies in the schools, candlelight vigils on the steps of city hall? *Please Lord, wake me up from this dream—this nightmare.*

****

My father received a phone call as we were leaving the service and we rushed home to meet Detective Padron who was waiting to speak with me. His squad car was already parked in our driveway when we arrived, with the driver's side door open. He stepped out of the car as soon as we drove past, notebook in hand. *Hurry Dad, we don't want to waste this man's precious time.*

Within minutes, I was seated on the couch in the living room between my parents while the detective sat across from us in a chair he had yanked from our dining room table. He was middle-aged, taller than my dad and a little pudgy around the edges. His thick neck led up to a head of spiky salt and pepper hair, which matched his gray eyes. He sat tall and rested his elbows on the wooden armrests, flicking a pen between his pointer and middle fingers.

"Now, uh, Miss White…" Detective Padron spoke my name as though he wasn't sure what I was actually called, looking down at his notebook and then back up at me.

"It's Lillian," I told him. "It's okay if you call me that."

I hoped for a moment that being on a first name basis would lighten his mood; perhaps then I wouldn't feel like a witness taking the stand against a criminal. But he nodded and continued his interrogation as if Brad was just some fugitive on the run.

"Lillian," he repeated. "I understand you were with Brad Lee on the evening of May sixteenth, is that correct?"

"Yes." *Am I supposed to elaborate?*

"And can you tell me when you last saw Brad?"

"He dropped me off at my front door at 9:59 pm."

The detective gave me a questioning glance.

"I remember it was that exact time because my curfew was ten o'clock and I was making sure I wasn't late." *Do I sound like I'm sucking up? Trying to come across like a goody-goody church girl who never misses a curfew?*

"So the last time you saw Brad he was leaving your front porch at *approximately* 10:00 pm?" He stressed approximately as though he wasn't buying my curfew line.

"Yes."

"And that is the last time you saw him before he was reported missing?"

"Yes." *No.* I was suddenly afraid to correct myself and tell him about Brad's visit to my window. Even with my parents sitting on either side of me, I was overcome with a wave of panic. *If I correct myself now he won't believe anything I say. But if I don't tell him, he will never know the difference...right?*

"Did Brad give you any indication of where he was going after he left your house?"

"He was going home."

"Brad wasn't going to any graduation parties or other festivities that night?"

*Stop using his name with that tone!*

"No, he was invited to a graduation party at Jason Hamilton's house but he didn't want to go." I glanced to my left to look at my dad, my eyes felt droopy and desperate like a hound dog. He gave me a quick nod then looked back at the Detective. I was on my own.

"Do you have any reason to think Brad would have wanted to harm himself?"

"What? No," I insisted, clearing my dry throat. "Not at all."

"To your knowledge, was Brad recently involved with any type of drugs or narcotics?" He held his pen to the paper, like it was his finger on the trigger of a gun, ready to fire.

"No, sir." I attempted to take a deep breath, but the air in our living room felt thick. "Brad is a good guy, he wasn't doing anything like that…" I suddenly began rambling like a faucet of words turned on full blast. "And that's why I just think something is really wrong. It's not like him to not communicate with anyone, especially with me. If he was going anywhere besides home he would have told me, and he definitely wasn't going to harm himself or to buy drugs or anything even remotely…"

"Miss White," Detective Padron interjected. "While I appreciate your desire to defend his character, his criminal record is telling us a different story."

Both of my parents shot me looks. Mom threw her hands over her mouth to hide her gasp.

"His criminal record?" My dad asked before I could speak. His eyes were turned towards the detective but I knew the question was meant for me.

"Yeah, Brad was involved in some harmless, childish

pranks…but he never told me anything about…" I trailed off, unsure how to end the sentence. My breath was leaving my body again. *This can't be happening.*

Detective Padron flipped a few pages back in his notebook. "I'm not at liberty to go into detail, but his juvenile record includes many crimes for which he was tried and found guilty. The most recent being November of…"

I didn't have to hear him finish. His last offense had occurred only days before our encounter in the snow. All Brad's stories about raiding refrigerators must have been a G-rated version of the past. I remembered what he said in front of the lake on Friday night, 'You saved my life.' *But what did I save him from?* A dry lump settled in the back of my throat as I rubbed his class ring between my fingers.

"That was a long time ago," I managed to say. "He's changed a lot since then."

"I certainly understand that, during adolescence, youth go through various stages of rebellion. But my point in asking this is to understand his current state of mind. Frankly, at this time we have no reason to assume that Brad has met with foul play or danger of any type, however, a possible drug relapse may have altered his state of mind and caused him to want to leave. There is just nothing leading us to believe he left involuntarily." *A drug relapse?*

"But I'm telling you," I insisted. "Brad doesn't do drugs. And he *wouldn't* have just left voluntarily. He had a job lined up for the summer, he's enrolled in the state college for the fall. We had made plans for the next day…" I was trailing off. It didn't matter what I said; the detective wasn't listening. Not to my words anyway.

"Miss White, I'm not sure you understand…"

"You need to talk to Lizard," I spit out, cutting him off. "Sorry."

"I'm sorry, did you say *Lizard*? Is this a classmate of Brad's?" He put his pen back to the paper, ready to write.

"Yes, uh, well no. He dropped out of school early in the year, now he has some car repair shop in an old barn off Highway Forty-one. Michael Lizardo, that's his real name, was a friend of Brad's before we were together. I haven't seen him since graduation, but he was upset with Brad on Friday night about missing Jason's party. I'm sure if you just talk to him…"

"Ah yes, Michael Lizardo," he said with a nod. "I've already spoken with him. In fact, he called the station to report that you have been harassing him."

I flew out of my seat. "*What?*"

"Have you been calling him repeatedly in an attempt to get information about Brad's whereabouts?"

"No!" I shrieked. "I mean, well yes, I called him a few times. But I called *everyone* I know!"

He motioned for me to sit back down, and I sunk down into the cushion between my parents. "I'm going to ask that you refrain from contacting Mr. Lizardo again."

I started to speak, but my mom placed her hand on my knee and gave it a squeeze.

"You need to let me do my job," the detective continued. "If Michael has information about Brad, it needs to come through me. I'm sure you understand." His inflection sounded like he was asking a question but the expression on his face indicated it was, in fact, a statement.

"Yes, sir." I nodded, squirming in my seat. *Why is he making me feel like I'm guilty of something? So I called the guy a few times, it's not a crime. And a far cry from harassment.*

"If you can give me a little more information about your relationship with Brad." His left eyebrow rose as he spoke, his jawbone clenching in and out as he waited for my response.

I peered out of the corner of my eye at my father who was staring at me. To my right my mother fiddled with her wedding band, her hands clasped as she held her gaze towards the detective. I didn't know where to start. *What is he asking me? Is he asking if we are sleeping together? That's none of his business. Even if I tell him we aren't, he probably wouldn't believe me. If he is convinced Brad is nothing more than a common criminal, does he think that he has hurt me in some way? Brad would never hurt me. He would never want me to hurt the way I hurt right now...*

"Lillian?"

I heard my name but it wasn't from the detective, it was my mom. She rested her hand on my back.

"Are you all right?" she asked. "Is this too much?"

"No, no. I'm fine." I shook my head. *Snap out of it.* "Brad and I have been dating for about six months." I tried to study Detective Padron's face. I couldn't read his vacant expression. He looked back at me for a long moment before retreating back to his notebook.

"Would you say you consider your relationship with Brad to be serious?"

I nodded. "He loves me." I glanced down at my hands and picked at the dry skin on the edges of my fingers. I didn't like how the words sounded when they reached my tongue, as though they were in his defense. *See, he's a good guy. He loves a good girl like me. Or does he...*

"And for how long has he been telling you that?"

"Well, not long."

"Define, 'not long'," Detective Padron said, his eyebrows furled.

"I mean, the first time he said he loved me was the night of graduation. When he brought me home."

He began writing again, more frantically than before.

"So, just to clarify, you are telling me the first time he told you he loved you was on your front porch the night he went missing?"

*Well, not exactly.* "Yes." I could feel my face growing red and hoped no one would notice. I didn't know how to explain why I had lied; it had been such a simple slip of the tongue that now felt like a blatant lie. But I couldn't take it back.

"Yet you do not believe that he planned to leave that night? Even though he was telling you this for the first time?" He wasn't asking, he was telling. He looked to my parents.

"Lillian," my mom cut in. "It does sound like he may have had other intentions behind what he said. Are you sure nothing seemed strange? You didn't get any feelings that he was trying to tell you..."

*Oh no. What have I done?*

"No!" I interjected. "We had a perfect picnic on the lake after graduation, it was just a really great night, that's *all*. He wasn't telling me he loved me as a goodbye. I'm positive."

Out of the corner of my eye, I watched my dad offer a

small nod to the detective. He closed his notepad and straightened his back. It was over.

"Lillian, that's all I need from you for today if you have told me everything." He cocked his head to the side as he spoke, undoubtedly some sort of police intimidation tactic. *It's not working.*

My mind raced back to the window, knowing it was my last chance to come clean. *But why is it important? It's nothing more than a minor detail...right? Or could the fact that he returned to the window to tell me he loved me instead of simply saying it on the front porch in some way de-bunk the premeditation story that the detective is so desperate to believe?* I knew my parents would hear 'he came to my window' and automatically assume I had made a nightly ritual of sneaking out, or worse, sneaking him in. I so desperately wanted to find Brad, to have him home, but I wondered if shedding light on this minor detail would only make me a victim of house arrest when (*if*) he returned?

"I think that's enough for now," Dad told him before I could say otherwise. "The past twenty-four hours or so have been really tough."

"I understand," he said. "Well, Lillian, you have been very helpful."

*No, I haven't. All I've done is add tick marks to your tally of reasons why you shouldn't waste your time looking for Brad.*

Detective Padron reached out to shake my parents' hands and motioned for mine last.

"Will you please talk to Lizard again?" I asked as my hand met his grasp. His grip was strong; my bony fingers were crushed up against one another as he squeezed.

"It only makes sense to speak with a man that willingly goes by the name of *Lizard*," he said with a condescending smile, revealing his surprisingly white teeth for the first time. "I'll be in touch."

My dad held the door for him as he left; Mom put her arm around my shoulders and pulled me close.

"I'm sure it's hard finding out Brad isn't who you thought he was. I'm sorry." She nodded to Dad and he headed into the kitchen, leaving us alone for a mother-daughter crisis talk.

"What? No." I pulled away from her grasp. "He isn't some criminal like the detective is making him out to be. You know him better than that!"

"And I would have liked to think that *you* know him better than that," Mom said. "But if he lied to you about having a criminal record then you have no idea what else he was lying to you about, Lillian." It was obvious this wouldn't be a comforting chat—it was a confrontation.

"He didn't lie about his past, Mom." *He wasn't truthful, either.* "I didn't *ask* him if he had a record. I don't care what happened before we were together, it doesn't matter!" *What are the lyrics to that old boy band song? I don't care where you've been or what you've done…it only matters if you love me…*

"Well then it sounds like you didn't want to know very much about him, did you?" Her tone dripped with condescension. "That is a very childish way of thinking. And if this relationship is as serious as you have made it out to be…. Lillian, I just hope you have not made any *big mistakes*."

"No!" I squealed. "This is completely unfair. Everyone is judging him and assuming the worst and he isn't here to defend himself. You're focusing on all the wrong things." I wanted to work up a few tears to help remind her what I was going through, but I couldn't and I wasn't sure why.

Mom stared at me silently, which didn't happen very often. After a long moment, her eyes broke away from mine and she shifted her gaze out the picture window as she spoke.

"Regardless of where Brad is now, I want you to think long and hard about how much you really know about him and what this relationship means. You are still young…"

"I'm seventeen!"

"Exactly," she said, turning her face towards me. "There is just so much that goes into a serious relationship and so many things you have to know about a person before you begin planning a future with them…"

"I know, Mom." I had to stop her. "We don't need to talk about this right now. All we need to do is find him. Please." I chewed on my thumbnail as I searched her eyes for any sign of compassion.

She let out a heavy sigh. "Just come and get some lunch."

Mom headed towards the kitchen, pushing her way through the swinging door that separated the rooms. The idea of sitting around the table with my family, listening to Graham and Eliza giggle and carry on without a care in the world, made me cringe.

"I'm not hungry," I told her through the door. "I'm going for a walk."

"Alone?" she asked emphatically, sticking her face in the doorway.

"Yeah. Who else am I going to go with?" *Not Brad.*

"I don't think that's a very smart thing to do. Not after all that has happened…"

"Mom!" I threw my hands in the air. "Two minutes ago you were convinced Brad ran away to become a drug dealer or something. Now you're telling me I can't even walk down my own street because he is missing?"

"Our street is exactly where he went missing *from*, Lillian," she said as she returned to the living room. "You need to consider your own safety."

"Wait. Are you saying you believe that something happened to him and he didn't just run away?" I asked. "Do you believe me?"

It took her a moment to answer. "I don't know, Lillian," she sighed. "I just don't know."

In the kitchen, I could hear Eliza relaying the details of craft time in that morning's Sunday school class to Dad and Graham. Mom looked towards the door with a long face.

"Just be careful," she finally said. "Take your phone."

"I will."

"I'll save you some casserole."

"Thanks, Mom." I nodded, not wanting to start another argument by telling her I had lost all traces of an appetite since Brad had disappeared.

Mom pulled me in for a long hug and stroked the back of my head as she held me. I had grown a few inches taller than her over the summer before eighth grade, but in that moment, I felt so small in her arms.

# 5

## unasked questions go unanswered

THE SUN WAS BRIGHT AND THE WARM BREEZE made the green leaves on the trees around our house dance as if celebrating the first Sunday of summer. It was a beautiful day; too beautiful for the occasion. It was the type of day Brad and I would have loved to spend at the lake with Anna and Thomas, swimming and laughing until the moon was high in the sky. But instead I was alone; walking down the street Brad vanished from as the police, my parents, and assumedly the rest of the town, were dragging his name through the mud.

The stretch of road that divided Anna's property line from mine was enveloped by dense rows of trees, their branches stretching high across the roadway and providing me with shade as I walked. Somewhere in this tunnel of foliage, Brad disappeared. He could have met with any fate that night that would have gone unseen by anyone on the other side of the trees. I knew the search groups had combed the area the night before, but I couldn't help but bring out my inner CSI. I looked for tire tracks, scraps of clothing, or broken branches that might signify some sort of accident or struggle. *If he was struck by a car, possibly a drunk driver leaving one of the local parties, he may have been tossed off the road into the ditch. The driver could have panicked and decided to force Brad into their vehicle and hold him somewhere to cover their tracks. Or...*

I tried to shake off the grimmer possibilities and think back to Friday night. *Did any cars drive by after Brad left?* If so, I hadn't bothered to notice. I had lain there thinking about Brad until I dozed off. *Who knows what could have been happening to Brad just a few hundred yards from my window while I was fast asleep.* The Lees had asked Anna whether she had seen anything that night since her house sat only a quarter mile from mine and past the wall of trees. But she had been at Thomas's until after eleven and then slept over at Tess' house across town. Anna's mom and stepdad claimed to have been asleep since just after nine o'clock, exhausted from the work week. The walls of Anna's house were potential witnesses, but of course, they wouldn't be talking.

I studied the ground next to the road, letting my eyes cover only a few square inches at a time. Grass, dirt, leaves, weeds, a scattering of small broken branches and twigs; nothing seemed out of the ordinary. Where were the size eleven footprints, ripped pieces of Brad's t-shirt, DNA covered cigarette butts, trace amounts of blood spatter? There wasn't so much as a crumpled beer can to be found. It just didn't make sense. *Where are you, Brad?*

A rustling sound came from behind the trees, causing the hair on my arms to stand on end. I stopped in my tracks and slowly turned my head around, thinking back to my mom's words of caution and safety.

"Hello?" I whimpered.

There was no answer, yet I couldn't shake the feeling that someone was watching me. I stood in the middle of the road, frozen, as I waited.

"Hello," I said again, more assertive this time. "Brad?"

I thought I heard a branch snap to my left but knew my mind was good at playing tricks on me. *Don't do this to yourself. Don't imagine him again.* I couldn't decide if I was imagining it was him, or someone—or something—else. *Or am I imagining it at all?* I took a few light steps toward the sound and waited again, holding my breath. I jumped as another rustling noise came from the same direction.

"Who's there?"

I considered parting the thick branches with my arms and attempting to see through to the other side, but I was afraid of what I might find. I made myself take one more step towards the tree line as the rustling became frantic and the sound moved quickly in the other direction, running away from where I stood. I wasn't sure what I wanted it to be. *A deer? A large rabbit? A barn cat? A bum living in the woods who is responsible for Brad's disappearance?* Or Brad himself…running from me because he knew I had learned his secrets.

Although I told myself it had been nothing but a small woodland creature, I took off in a sprint towards my house. I no longer felt safe on my quiet street in my small town with Brad gone. This place where I had grown up and made so many memories was now a potential crime scene. And the person who was supposed to protect me was gone without a trace.

****

Once I was safely inside my bedroom, I called the Lees and we spoke at length regarding what to do next. I didn't ask about Brad's criminal history, although I wasn't sure if it was because I didn't want to upset them by bringing it up or because I didn't want to know the truth. Mrs. Lee invited me over to their house and I borrowed Mom's SUV instead of attempting another walk down the dismal roadway.

I had imagined that I would see reporters camped out on their front lawn, waiting with microphones at bay like guns in a Wild West duel. But instead, the house was quiet, eerily so. Brad's silver two-door truck that I had grown to love was parked in the driveway in its usual spot, with splatters of mud around the wheel well. On Saturday mornings, he would always hose off any debris from the week prior, yet today was Sunday and the brown residue was baking in the sun. *He would never leave his truck like this on purpose.*

As I waited on the front steps for an answer to my timid knocking, I glanced at my surroundings. There were no undercover cops sitting in dark cars staking out the premises, no colorful ribbons tied around trees. Everything appeared to be normal, even though just inside the brick and mortar of the Lee residence a family was hurting, missing an intricate piece of their puzzle.

"Hi, Lillian," young Montana said as she greeted me at the front door.

"Hi, sweetie," I said as I gave her a quick hug. "How are you?"

"I'm all right I guess," she said with a shrug. "Everyone is pretty sad around here."

"I know. It's sad at my house too."

Mrs. Lee, or Janice as she had asked me to call her, came into the entryway and offered me a tired smile that didn't reach her eyes. "Come on in, Lillian. Thanks for coming."

She tussled Montana's hair. "Why don't you go see if Daddy needs help with the posters, okay sweetheart?"

"Yes, ma'am." Montana nodded and headed towards the kitchen. "Bye, Lillian," she said over her shoulder.

"I'll see you later."

Janice owned an interior design business, and the home reflected her work. Perfectly placed accent furniture hugged the cream-colored walls in the foyer. I let my fingertips drag the wooden railing as she led me upstairs and through a dim hallway that led to Brad's bedroom.

"I thought this might help," she said as we climbed the carpeted steps.

The door was closed as if his room had been quarantined off from the rest of the house. She grabbed the handle and swung it open as a burst of cool, fresh air escaped from inside. I had been in this room dozens of times yet without Brad in it, it seemed unfamiliar. The deep blue walls were covered in generic posters and paintings that were dispersed evenly around the room. I had never noticed how impersonal the décor was—it was almost as though the Lees had purchased the floor model of a teenage boy's bedroom.

Brad's bed was made, although the checkered comforter was crooked and crumpled in the corners like it had been quickly tossed over the mattress. The backpack he had carried with him to school every day, and sometimes to our picnics in the park, was propped neatly against his desk instead of strewn onto the floor as it typically would have been. The photo of us at prom rested in a brown frame that lay on its back on his nightstand, carelessly pushed over or shoved out of the way. My heart sank as I stared at the picture.

"The police went through his room yesterday, just to look for anything…suspicious," Janice said as she noticed my eyes on the photo. She picked it up and stood it upright. "They tried to put everything back in place but I'm sure they just knocked this over."

I nodded as I continued to examine the space. I had hoped I would be overcome with Brad's presence, yet I couldn't feel him in this room. His bedroom might as well have been a hotel room where he once stayed. *What else did the police touch?*

"You're welcome to spend as much time in here as you'd like." Janice motioned towards the bed as she parked herself on the mattress next to the footboard. "I must have sat on his bed for an hour this morning. It's just so hard not knowing what to do and where to look for him. Being in here was the only peace I could find."

"Thanks."

I pulled the rolling chair out from in front of Brad's black desk and sat down gently. I couldn't bring myself to sit on the bed next to his mom. It would have seemed like we were mourning him. We sat in silence for several minutes, both of us scanning the room and searching for obvious clues of Brad's whereabouts. I thought back to the countless crime TV shows I watched in the afternoons. There weren't any obvious trapdoors cut out in the wooden floor, no paintings with moving eyeballs or symbolic maps with push pins connected by string hanging on the walls. If Brad had intended to leave behind some kind of mystery for us to solve, it wasn't evident in this room.

I bit my tongue for as long as I could but my curiosity was getting the best of me. "What was Brad arrested for?" I blurted.

Janice shook her head and sighed. "Oh, Lillian. I guess he didn't tell you."

"No." I shrugged. "But the detective did."

"He had quite a troubled childhood. He went through a lot—a lot more than any child should have to go through," she said. "And after we moved here, when Brad was in sixth grade, he just seemed to fall into the wrong crowd."

"With Lizard?"

"Well, yes, and Jones. And there were a few other odd-named kids who came and went. As he got older he started racking up a list of misdemeanors…vandalism, burglary, disturbing the peace, those types of crimes. He must have a served over a hundred community service hours by the time it was all said and done."

"How is it possible I never heard about any of this when it happened?" I asked. *It seems like the whole town knows within minutes when someone gets a bad haircut, let alone arrested.*

"There are certain laws that protect minors from being exploited by the media, and Brad's father's friendship with Judge Hawthorn certainly helped. We've been working on getting his records expunged now that he is eighteen, so he can start college with a clean slate."

"So it all goes away?"

She nodded. "In theory, yes. But certain crimes are really hanging over his head in this investigation. Although he pleaded not guilty, he was tried for drug possession and grand theft auto..."

"Wait, he stole a car?" My jaw dropped as I pictured Brad huddled under a steering wheel, frantically trying to cross wires like something out of an action movie. I tried to shake the image away.

"He claimed he was just *in* the car and was not the one who had stolen it, but who knows..." her voice trailed off.

I wanted to ask about the troubled childhood she had mentioned but stopped myself. I was afraid it would only make me seem like I knew even less about the guy I was claiming to be in love with. *Why didn't he tell me all of this? What was he protecting me from? Or protecting himself from?*

"The police have a theory that Brad has stolen a car and that is what he used to leave town," Janice continued as she dug her fingers into her forehead.

"But if he wanted to leave, why wouldn't he take his own

truck that's parked in your driveway?"

"They say that would have been too easy for them to trace. If he is in a stolen vehicle they have a tougher time narrowing down the search."

Suddenly my mind raced back to the night of graduation. We always took Brad's truck when we went out, yet that night he had suggested I borrow my dad's car.

*"I can give you another lesson on driving a stick shift,"* he had said.

He let me drive to the lake, keeping his hand on mine on top of the shift and helping me navigate the grooves between gears. But on the way home he took the keys and sat in the driver's seat without a word otherwise. I had been far too wrapped up in the mood of the evening to notice or care at the time, but now it seemed strange. *Why didn't we just take the truck? What were you trying to tell me, Brad?*

"Do they have a record of cars in the area being stolen the night Brad…disappeared?" I asked anxiously.

"From what I understand there were no vehicles reported missing on Friday night, but there were several in the weeks prior…which is furthering their theory that his disappearance was pre-meditated."

*And I certainly didn't disprove this theory when I dropped the 'I love you' bomb.*

"Mrs. Lee, uh, Janice, what do you think? Where do you think he is?" I looked deep into her eyes as I asked, unsure if I even wanted her answer.

"I think…" she swallowed. "I think you and I both know a different side of Brad than what those police reports say."

I nodded. *Good answer.*

"But I also think," she continued. "That Brad has a lot of secrets."

I wished I could argue that she was wrong; that he never kept secrets from me. Up until the past few days, I always thought Brad had made me his world and confided his innermost thoughts to me. Yet suddenly complete strangers seemed to know things about him that I had never heard or imagined. I had painted a picture of his past in my mind based on the facts he had given me, but now there were holes in the canvas. All I knew was the fairy tale version of the story that he had fabricated.

"Lillian, I just want you to know that despite everything that has come out about Brad, we will do everything we can to find him. There's nothing any police officer can say that will convince us to stop looking for him."

"Thank you." I planted the palms of my hands onto Brad's desk and pressed them onto the cold black metal. I wanted to feel him but instead, all I felt were my palms growing sticky against the desktop. *I need answers.*

****

The Lees and I planned informal search parties for the coming days, knowing that police involvement would be minimal, and sought out news coverage. But Brad's face only ran once on the four o'clock news—with a thirty-second spot requesting if anyone had seen him to call the local police department. They received several calls, mostly mistaken identity or pranks, but there was minimal follow-up. If he had been a young child or a beautiful girl he would have undoubtedly been more important to the media. But to them, he was just another eighteen-year-old runaway with a dodgy past. It didn't matter to the media who he really was, or what he was leaving behind.

I spent the first two weeks of my summer vacation searching for Brad, in woods, ditches, creeks and along the side of the interstate. Our initial search parties were huge, with over one hundred people turning out to 'help bring him home'. But as the days went on and we found nothing but broken bottles and crumpled fast food bags, the numbers grew less and less. I didn't know what we were even looking for. I never expected to find Brad lying in a field or a drainage ditch, but it felt like we were supposed to check.

The Lees poured over Brad's cell phone records, only to discover there had been no calls made to mysterious numbers and no 'pings' on local towers from the night he disappeared because his battery had been dead. A call to the bank informed them that the debit card he carried in his wallet hadn't been used since the day before graduation, and no large sums of money had been withdrawn. *Another dead end.* We were going through the motions, following all the suggestions you can find on the Internet for how to locate your missing loved one, but it seemed forced. And it became exhausting.

Pastor Allen's wife organized a prayer meeting one Tuesday morning and a few dozen people from town showed up to hold hands and share their prayers for Brad. I had trouble finding the words to say when the person next to me squeezed my fingers, signaling my turn to speak. I had prayed every day, or attempted to, but my words constantly turned to frustration and then into anger. *How could you let this happen to him—to me? How many times will I pray this same prayer, asking for Brad to be found, without resolution?* The weight on my chest became a barrier between my thoughts and my prayers; I was angry with God. As much as I wanted to believe that I would ask and receive, I was no longer convinced. I didn't feel like He was listening, much like the rest of the town.

The posters baked in the summer sun, causing the glimmer in Brad's deep blue eyes to fade away. He was truly becoming just another face on a missing poster; one you glance at when you enter the grocery store or the post office but never bother to study the information or care who that person is, or was. The Lees created a social media page for Brad that was updated frequently in the beginning, notifying the town of upcoming searches and possible sightings. They posted a video they had made, along with young Montana, assuring him they loved him no matter what kind of trouble he may be in and that they just wanted him to come home. I was tempted to make my own video, hoping that if he saw my face and heard me saying how much I loved and missed him that somehow he would find his way back home. But I quickly realized that if he was somewhere he could search the web and watch viral videos, it meant his absence was likely intentional and nothing I said was going to matter.

As the weeks without Brad went on, my energy and stamina continued to drain until I felt completely lost. The search parties dwindled to one search every few days, and the people around me began to resume life as usual. Anna and Thomas planned trips to the lake with our group of friends and I would hear them laughing and shouting as they drove by my house with the windows down, enjoying the summer breeze. I was always invited, but after a while it became more of a formality than an actual invitation. They knew I wouldn't come. I couldn't go on as though Brad had just never existed, and I wouldn't allow myself to spend an afternoon with our friends in the sun if he wasn't there.

Every time a smile tried to creep to the corners of my mouth I told myself I was betraying him. My heart hurt, like another brick was strapped to my chest for every day, or every hour, he was gone.

I saw him everywhere. His face appeared on the body of any blond-haired boy or man I passed in the street. I was tempted to grab the shoulder of every male I walked behind and spin him around to examine his face; to search for any sign of Brad behind the eyes. Every time I fell asleep he was there in my dreams. Sometimes I was reliving our date at the lake and in other dreams I screamed as I watched his decomposing body being pulled from the water by a large crane. In one nightmare he was walking through the hallway at school and when I called his name he turned towards me and yelled, "Leave me alone, Lillian. I don't love you." All I wanted to do was lay in bed, yet I didn't want to fall asleep. I was treading emotional water, exhausted but unable to relax for fear I would drown.

When it came time for our annual family vacation in Florida, I refused to take the trip. Mom was hurt, Dad was angry, and I was a mess. I had already skipped the Honors Choir retreat in the Blue Ridge Mountains, insisting I couldn't bear the thought of leaving town in case he was found, and this time was no different. They let me stay with Anna after much debating and yelling back and forth, but soon after they left I realized I felt more alone than ever.

Anna spent nights on the phone with Thomas, whispering once she thought I fell asleep. I let her talk me into going to a Fourth of July party at Mandy's, desperate to appear normal again, but regretted the decision the moment I arrived. I could feel people watching me as I sat huddled on the front steps of Mandy's house, clutching my phone and waiting for Anna to give me a ride. My classmates whispered about me between blasts from fireworks, thinking I couldn't hear them but their voices carried through the night breeze.

"What's her deal?"

"Wow, she looks terrible. Maybe Brad took one look at her and ran away."

"I don't know what he ever saw in her, anyway. He was way too hot for her!"

"That's what she gets for dating a convict…"

"Stop it, you guys," a girl from my choir class hissed. "I feel so bad for her."

I didn't want to cry in front of them, but my eyes that had been dry for weeks suddenly filled with tears. I dropped my face into my hands.

"You okay?"

Sniffling, I looked up to see a brown-haired boy standing a few feet away.

"Sorry, dumb question," he sat beside me on the step. "Clearly you're not okay."

I quickly wiped the tears from under my eyes with the tips of my fingers. "I'm fine."

"Do you want to talk about it?"

There was a sudden *boom* as fireworks lit up the yard. His eyes caught the flicker of light and my heart dropped. They were sad eyes, attempting to hide behind the dark strands of hair that fell in his face, but they were blue. *Brad blue.*

"No," I said over the crackle of the fireworks. "I really don't. Sorry."

He stood up and brushed off the back of his ripped jeans with his hand. "No need to be sorry."

"Wait," I said as he turned to leave. "I know you."

"You do?" He stopped in his tracks.

"You were at my house...the night of the first search party. I saw you in my yard."

"Oh." He nodded. "Right. I hope it's okay I was there. I just wanted to help."

The corners of my mouth turned up in a small smirk. "Seems to be your theme."

"At least I'm good for something," he said as he smiled. His eyes lit up again and I had to look away. "I'll see you around."

"Yeah." I bit at my thumbnail. "See ya."

My face grew warm as he walked away and I batted my eyelashes through oncoming teardrops. There was always something that reminded me of Brad. As the tears streamed faster I realized I was no longer breaking down. I was officially broken.

# 6

## bring me back to life

IT HAD BEEN THREE MONTHS AND THIRTEEN days but it might as well have been years, or centuries even. Thousands of posters were distributed and just as many hours were spent searching to no avail. I had grown numb. The only thing I could feel was a constant, throbbing pain in my heart, intermixed with bouts of anger and denial.

Despite what everyone said, no one understood what losing Brad was like. People can only understand things they have experienced, and sometimes not even then. A break-up, a divorce, even death; the pain of these events had been experienced by practically everyone around me. But no one understood the way it felt *not knowing*. I needed answers.

I needed resolution. I needed *closure*. No matter what the truth was.

I forced myself out of bed and planted my feet on the cool wood floor. I had been dreading this day for weeks. For my friends, senior year meant being one step closer to freedom. But for me, it meant walking the halls as 'that girl who dated the missing guy'. *That girl who completely let herself go. That girl who lied to the police.* I couldn't wait to see what superlative I received in the yearbook.

I glanced at the stack of sheet music that sat in the corner of my room, collecting dust along with my un-touched acoustic guitar. Singing had been one of my favorite past times since I was young, and I had become a strong vocalist over the past few years. Yet now, ever since the morning after graduation, the thought of opening my mouth in song made me cringe. Getting out of choir practice at church had been easy—I simply stopped showing up and no one asked questions. But avoiding music in school was going to be a different story. I didn't know what would come out if I tried to sing again, and I was doomed to find out in third period Honors Choir.

As I brushed my teeth, I could smell Mom's buttermilk pancakes sizzling on the griddle, accompanied by bacon being fried. As usual, I wasn't hungry. Outside my door, Graham and Eliza tore down the hallway to the kitchen. I wondered how they always had so much energy in the morning. I couldn't remember the last time I had that kind of childlike enthusiasm. I pulled on a pair of capris from off of the floor and thumbed through my closet for a top to wear, landing thoughtlessly on a flannel button-down. *One arm at a time, one button at a time.* Brad's ring still hung on the chain around my neck, but I tucked it inside the collar of the shirt.

I took a long look in the mirror. I had tan lines from days of searching in the noon sun, yet my skin had never been so dull and lifeless. I secretly hoped that people would see right through me, like a translucent being that no one bothered to notice. As I stared at my reflection, I tried to tell myself to shake the negativity. This was my senior year, focusing in on the event that my friends and I had been looking forward to since the first day of freshman orientation. *Why can't I just be excited?* I had known I'd be entering this year alone as Brad would be at college. But the type of alone I was feeling was nothing that I could have prepared for.

"Dear Lord," I whispered, squeezing my eyelids shut. "Please find him. Help me. Save me. Anything…" I shook my head. It was useless.

Crouched on the floor, I fished around with one hand under my bed for my book bag. I stretched my arm farther and the tips of my fingers brushed the wooden box I had stored beneath the bed frame months ago, attempting to forget it was there. *Deep breath in, deep breath out.* My fingers lingered for a moment, and before I could stop myself I was pulling the small treasure chest from its hiding place. It was perfectly made, carved from a log of driftwood Brad had smuggled back from our trip to Topsail Island over spring break. The letters 'L&B' were burned into the top of the box. I allowed my fingers to trace the indentions as I had many times since May seventeenth.

With a deep breath, I lifted the corners of the lid and set it on the floor beside me. I stared at the folded love notes, candid photos and ticket stubs I had carefully preserved over the course of the six months I had spent with Brad. The dried corsage from my junior prom lay across the top and dozens of tiny dead buds were scattered amongst the contents. These once sentimental, romantic reminders now seemed like the Cliff Notes of our tainted relationship, housed in a small, dark, wooden coffin. *Maybe I should bury it.*

"Lillian! Breakfast!" Mom's call echoed through the hall.

I shoved the box back to its hiding place and gathered my notebooks into my arms. As I rose to my feet I glanced out the window for any sign of Anna's blue compact car coming to take me to school. I could easily predict how the morning's conversation with my parents would play out; I knew I'd need a quick getaway.

I crept down the hallway and slipped into the kitchen behind my mother who was bent over the sink, up to her elbow in soapsuds. But I wasn't stealthy enough, and she quickly turned her head towards me.

"Well good morning, Senior!" she said, wiping her hands on a towel that sat on the countertop beside her.

"Good morning," I groaned, hovering in the doorway.

"Come on, have a seat. I've got a whole stack of pancakes waiting for you." She pulled a chair away from the round table in the middle of the room and motioned towards it emphatically. Graham and Eliza sat across from each other, shoveling forkfuls of syrup-covered pancakes into their mouths.

"Thanks, Mom. But I'm really not hungry," I insisted.

"Oh Lillian, sit down. You've got to eat something, you look terrible."

"Well, thanks," I said flatly as I sunk into a chair.

"I'm sorry, I didn't mean it like that." She dropped three pancakes onto my plate as she spoke and drizzled them in a honey colored syrup. "You just look so nice when you have some makeup on, and I love how you used to do your hair."

I grunted, thinking back to the time when I was thirteen and she made me wash off my mascara before I was allowed to leave the house. *I wish I could be thirteen again.*

"Lillian, did you like fifth grade? My friend Emily Myers said that her big brother said it was the worst grade of all," seven-year-old Eliza stated innocently. "I told Graham he is gonna hate it but he doesn't believe me."

"I'm only gonna hate it if there's lots of homework," Graham said with his mouth full. "Do you remember if there was lots of homework in fifth grade, Lil?"

*Fifth grade. Brad.*

"I…" I pictured Brad chasing after me in the gym. "I don't remember much about fifth grade," I lied. "But be nice to the girls, okay?"

"Nice to the girls?" He wrinkled his nose, still chewing. "Yeah, right."

"I bet Graham has a girlfriend!" Eliza giggled. "Do you, Graham? Do you have a girlfriend?"

"Eliza, Graham, if the two of you are done why don't you see if Dad is ready to leave?" Mom interrupted.

They looked up at her, nodded, and rushed out of the

room, leaving their dirty dishes on the table. This must have been the cue. My eyes dropped to my plate.

"Lillian, I know this has been a hard summer for you, I do," she began once we were alone. "I just want to make sure you don't lose focus."

*"Focus on what, exactly?"* I wanted to ask, but I held my tongue and stabbed the prongs of my fork in and out of the gooey stack of pancakes in front of me. "I know, Mom," was all I managed to say.

"Did you get started on that application to Meredith yet? Early admission deadline is coming up fast. It would be a real weight off of your shoulders if you had a plan this early on…"

*I did have a plan, and it was nothing like this.* I dropped my fork onto my plate.

"Mom, we've talked about this. I'm not even sure if I want to go to college next year." I pushed the plate away from me and sunk deeper into my chair. "I just can't handle all of this right now."

Mom let out an audible sigh. "Lillian, as I've told you many times, I know what you're going through…"

"But you don't, Mom!" I cried. "Why can't you stop pretending you understand what this is like!" My voice was elevated and shrill. I wanted the words to come out as a scream but I only had the energy to muster up a high-pitched whine.

Mom opened her mouth to speak, taking in a large breath as her lips parted, but let out a heavy sigh instead. I took a small sip of milk from the plastic tumbler in front of me before pushing my chair back from the table. As I stooped for my backpack I heard her gently clear her throat.

"You can't throw away your future because of a boy, Lillian," she insisted. "Your life does not have to stop because of this."

*Too late, it already did.*

"Your Dad and I care deeply for the entire Lee family, but Detective Padron was quite clear about Brad's past. You have *no idea* what sort of trouble he might have gotten himself into, or what kind of person he was before you…"

I heard a soft 'beep' from outside. *Saved by the horn.*

"That's Anna." I hurled my backpack over my shoulder and headed towards the side door. "I've got to go."

"Lillian, come straight home after school," she called after me. "We aren't finished talking."

I stopped in the doorway, turned back and hurriedly nodded. Wherever Brad was, whomever he was with, I wished they would come back for me too. It was hard to imagine a fate worse than not knowing.

Anna tapped her fingers against the steering wheel of the running car, bobbing her head to the pop song that played over the radio. A pink, rose-shaped air freshener swung back and forth from the rearview mirror. Her freshly chopped brown hair was pulled behind her ears and she hid her hazel eyes behind large sunglasses as she sat in the driver seat waiting for me. I made my way to the passenger door and gave her a small smile, slinging my bag into the backseat.

"Good morning, Darling," she said in a British accent as I pulled the seatbelt across my body.

"You got here just in time. I couldn't handle another

college speech this morning."

"Sorry, it took me forever to figure out what to wear."

Anna was dressed to impress, as always, in coral skinny jeans with a flowing off-white tank top, accented by gold costume jewelry that jingled around her wrists and neck. I glanced down at my oversized flannel shirt; I was already beginning to sweat in the August heat.

"Please tell me you slept last night, Lil," Anna said knowingly, keeping her eyes on the rearview mirror as she backed out of my driveway.

"Yes...I rested."

"Well, how are you doing? I feel like I haven't seen you in weeks. Are you ready to go back to school?" She pulled the car onto the street and sped towards the distant stop sign at the end of our quiet road.

"No," I sighed. *Not that I have much of a choice.*

"I'm sorry. I miss him too," she said softly. "Even though he graduated...it's going to be weird. Without him, I mean." She briefly took her eyes off the road to exchange a look of comfort. "I know today is probably going to suck. But I'm here for you, okay? We all are."

****

The Lions Port High parking lot was bustling with our classmates as we pulled in, some chatting with friends on the sidewalk while others made their way to their first-period classrooms. Anna jerked the car into her assigned spot—right beside Tess Janning's brand new convertible that her parents had bought for her as an early graduation present. She turned off the engine and looked at me as she unbuckled her seatbelt.

"Day one," she said, offering a cheesy, oversized grin. "Only one hundred and sixty-three more to go. Yes, I counted."

I let out a little grunt in place of a laugh. I reached to the back seat to retrieve my book bag as Anna let the drivers side door slam behind her. She and Tess began chatting loudly outside the window, complimenting each other on their tan skin and outfit choices. Just as I turned to exit the car, my eyes caught the rearview mirror. Behind Anna's compact, an empty parking space sat ominously. Brad's spot had been untouched all summer, preserving the skid marks from his truck tires as the pavement and spray painted numbers '861' faded in the sun.

I pulled a small tube of cherry lip balm from my pocket and removed the cap, watching the wax rise as I twisted the plastic gear on the bottom. I stared at myself in the rearview, rubbing the red balm across my dry lips before my focus shifted again to the parking space behind me. A truck raced into the spot and the vibrations from the bass guitar that played through the speakers shook me in my seat. I caught my breath and squinted to make out the driver and passenger. As my eyes focused on the truck I realized what I was looking at—there in the passenger seat sat a prettier, happier version of myself, applying lip gloss and laughing next to Brad.

Brad reached towards me and brushed the hair out of my face before he grabbed my cheeks and pulled me towards him. I watched him plant a deep kiss on my freshly glossed lips and I could almost feel his embrace. I closed my eyes and tried to imagine he was beside me again, only in Anna's car instead of his silver truck. But I jumped at the sudden honk of a horn, snapping my eyes open as my fantasy evaporated. I held my breath and as a black SUV appeared in the mirror and pulled into the empty parking spot I had been captivated by moments before.

"Hey there, hot stuff!" Thomas shouted to Anna as he leaned out the driver's side window of the SUV.

I sighed and ducked my head to exit the car, gently shutting the door behind me. Tess and Anna stood gossiping behind the bumper. Tess turned towards me with a smile, showing off the blonde tips she had added to her dark locks over the summer.

"Lillian, I thought you were going to spend homeroom in the car!" she exclaimed with a laugh. "What took you so long?"

I shrugged my shoulders and looked towards Thomas as he watched us from behind the tinted windshield.

"It's just Thomas, Lil," Anna said. "I'm sorry, I forgot to tell you he was assigned to Brad's space. He was planning to park in the gravel lot, out of respect for Brad, but then his first-period class got changed to the east wing and it just doesn't make much sense for him to walk from the exact opposite end of the building..."

"And I know Brad is still missing, Lil," Tess interjected. "But he wouldn't have been parking here, anyway. Because he graduated, I mean."

Anna's eyes searched mine for a reaction but my expression was blank. I didn't want to admit that Tess was right. The SUV continued to run as Thomas sat inside it, watching us.

"I really am sorry, Lil...we told him it was okay, but we

should have talked to you first..." Anna trailed on.

"It's fine," I finally said. "You're right. Brad doesn't go here anymore."

Our eyes locked for a moment before I looked to Thomas and gave him a nod. In response, the hum of the black SUV went silent and Thomas stepped out.

"Hey Lil," he said, extending one arm to hug me. "How are you?"

"I'm here," I grunted. *What am I supposed to say? Oh, I'm fine, great actually, thanks for asking?*

Thomas laid a quick smack on Anna's lips and motioned towards the school. "All right, ladies. Shall we?"

Mandy, followed closely by her summer fling Parker Felton, rushed to join Tess and Thomas as they headed for the side entrance to the building. The group went on chatting and laughing like normal high school seniors who hadn't lost a peer just months earlier. I had known coming back to school would be hard, but nothing could have prepared me for the utter happiness that was occurring all around me. Dragging my feet, I tried to follow the group, but I felt as though I was sinking into the pavement.

"Hey, are you sure it's okay?" Anna asked, hanging back. "I can tell Thomas it's not going to work out and he can just park in the other lot, it's really no problem at all. He won't care..."

"No, no." I shook my head. "Thanks, though. It's fine." *It is just a parking space, after all. If all I have left of Brad is a patch of black asphalt then things are worse than I thought.*

"I knew you'd be cool," Anna said as she nudged me with her elbow. "Now come on, Lil. Everything's going to be fine.

We're almost out of here! Senior year!"

I nodded and forced a tight-lipped smile, watching as she rushed towards the open doors. Anna joined our group inside the building, leaving me alone on the other side. I stopped for a moment and took a deep breath as the students around me funneled into the school like livestock. I took my first step onto the concrete floor of the east wing just as a shrill bell rang from above my head. The doors behind me swung shut. I was trapped in my own little educational nightmare.

Anna and Thomas rushed through the crowded hallway and I found myself lost in a pool of students. I'd had many nightmares about this exact scene. Sometimes I was naked and other times I was disfigured, but in every dream I was alone and surrounded by eyeballs. I walked towards my homeroom, knowing I was fully clothed, yet I still felt so exposed.

A girl I had sat beside in Geometry the year before, Cadence Campbell, stood by the wall and kept her eyes locked on me as I moved. The moment I looked her way she snapped her head towards her locker to avoid my gaze. I let out a heavy sigh. The hallway chatter was loud but I could still make out sentences that seemed to be about me.

"Wow, she's actually here."

"You know, they still don't know what happened to that guy."

"I was lab partners with Brad last year. Lillian's nice, but something always seemed a little off with him."

"Poor thing."

"Wow, is that really her?" one girl asked her friend. "She

looks terrible!"

I was no longer normal to my peers. In fact, I wasn't even Lillian anymore. I was just 'that girl who knew the missing guy.' *And yes, 'knew'.* Brad wasn't referred to in the present tense.

\*\*\*\*

I spent first period in a daze. Mr. Liner, my homeroom teacher, went over important dates coming up on the school calendar, including the fall formal and the last day for students to pay club dues, and passed out letters to our parents about scheduling senior photos. He offered me a flyer with information on auditions for the drama society's upcoming musical, but I didn't accept it.

"Don't you usually like to perform, Miss White?" he asked.

"I used to," I told him. "I'm just not into it anymore."

"That's a shame," he said as he sat the flyer back on his desk.

*You're telling me.*

After walking like a zombie down the halls, I made it to second-period calculus and aimlessly scribbled illegible notes in an old notebook from the year before. As I flipped the page I discovered a forgotten handwritten note on a blue shred of construction paper that I had slipped into the notebook that spring.

*Hey Lillian! Get back to work! XOXO*

I remembered the exact moment I received the note, and how I had blushed when I found it tucked in the pages of my textbook. Brad and I had gotten together the night before to study for the history class we took together, and we sat on my living room floor with books and flashcards strewn across the carpet, doing much more laughing and flirting than studying. I never needed much help in world history anyway, but a study date meant an opportunity to spend a school night together without a hassle from my parents. When I discovered the note before the test the next day I had looked across the classroom at Brad and he gave me a wink. I loved how special it was to share a private moment with him in a room full of people.

"Lillian?"

I heard my name and just as I glanced across the room I saw him. There sat Brad only a few desks over, looking back at me and smiling. *He wasn't gone after all; he's been here all along!* His smile was peaceful and content and I wanted to jump out of my chair and wrap my arms around him, never letting go. I smiled back as he tossed his shaggy blond hair out of his face without breaking his eyes away from mine.

"Lillian?"

I heard a voice again, but this time it was a woman's voice. I looked back towards to front of the classroom to find my teacher standing above my desk.

"Lillian, can you solve the equation?"

"What?"

I glanced towards the white board behind her head at the complicated math problem before looking back to Brad. There in his place sat another blond-haired guy, staring at me with a puzzled look on his face. I suddenly thought I was going to be sick.

"The equation on the board…"she said again. "Lillian, are you okay?"

My breathing became heavy as I fought back a panic attack. *I can't do this. I knew I couldn't do this. Why did everyone think I could do this?* My eyes filled with tears and the milk I had forced down for breakfast was quickly making its way back up into my throat.

"I'm sorry. I just need some air."

I snatched my book bag from under the desk and shoved my notebook inside, stumbling over my own feet as I rushed out of the room. I could feel the entire class's eyes on me as I pushed the door open and fell out into the hallway. *I have to get out of here.* I raced through the empty halls towards the first exit I could find until I was alone in the daylight outside the school walls. I was free, yet still trapped in the true story of my life.

I stopped for a moment to realize what I was doing. I had never cut class in my entire career as a student; in fact, I was rarely even tardy. But I wasn't the same person I had once been. *How can I be the same person when a part of me is missing? How can anyone expect me to be the same straight-A student after what I have gone through the past few months? How can they think I can walk down those halls and not see his face everywhere I turn?* I was suddenly overcome with the desire to run—run and leave it all behind. I tightened the straps of my backpack over my shoulders and took off into the parking lot. *Destination – anywhere but here.*

# 7

## relationship status: it's complicated

ONCE I REACHED THE BUSY DOWNTOWN STREET
I stopped to catch my breath, leaning my hands against my
knees as I panted. *Deep breath in, deep breath out.* When I looked
up I found myself in front of Crayborn's Hardware Store, the
neon sign blinking at me. Brad had worked there for the past
few years, keeping the shelves stocked and assisting the locals
who spent their afternoons picking out correctly sized screws
and new wrenches. Mr. Crayborn was behind the counter,
placing materials into a brown paper bag. He noticed me
through the glass. He nodded and gave me a smile.

Seeing the familiar shelves of the store, I was suddenly
overwhelmed with the desire to call Detective Padron; it had

been weeks since I had heard anything from him. I fished my cell phone from my pocket but the screen was black. The battery was dead after failing to charge it the night before. I backed away from the hardware store window and headed towards the diner I had frequented with Brad in search of a phone.

Inside the nostalgic fifties-style restaurant, the sweet scent of deep-fried dough and fresh baked desserts filled my nostrils. The aroma was overwhelming, but I wasn't hungry. I leaned across the stainless steel counter as a wrinkled, frizzy-haired waitress came towards me.

"Hi there honey, what can I get you?" she asked, pulling a small notepad and pen from the breast pocket of her ruffled apron.

"I just need to use the phone."

"Well certainly, sugar. Assuming it's a local call. My boss gets real annoyed when we call long distance," she replied with a chuckle as she lifted an old-fashioned, teal colored dial phone from beneath the counter.

"Yes, Ma'am." I nodded, reaching for it.

"Bet you gotta call your sweetheart, don't ya?" she asked with a wink.

"No, Ma'am," I whispered, sliding the phone towards me. The waitress backed away as I dialed. I had memorized the number three and a half months ago.

After three rings, a gruff voice picked up. "Morris County Police Department."

I could barely hear him over the bustling noise in the background.

"Yes, Detective Padron, please. Tell him it's Lillian White. I'm calling regarding Brad Lee's case." I held my hand over the mouth of the phone, hoping the other dining customers wouldn't overhear. On the stool to my left, an older gentleman was peering at me over his newspaper.

"Yeah, hold on," the man on the other end of the line said. Muffled jazz music played over the speaker as I waited.

The hanging bell on the door chimed and I turned to see the blue-eyed boy from the Fourth of July party entering the diner. He looked more rugged than I remembered, his dark locks of hair hung in his face and he wore a tattered gray hooded sweatshirt. His eyes caught mine as he walked by but I quickly looked past him at another familiar face. Hanging behind his head was one of Brad's faded posters, tacked to a cluttered bulletin board between colorful business cards and advertisements. The poster asked the ominous question, *have you seen this man?*

"Miss White?" Detective Padron came on the line, answering from a much quieter room. I cleared my throat and pressed the mouthpiece close to my face.

"Hello, Detective Padron. It's just Lillian, I wanted to check in. Is there any new information? About Brad, I mean. Anything you can tell me?"

"No new leads. Few and far between, in fact." His voice dripped with boredom as if I was calling about a missing wallet or a kitten stranded in a tree.

I sighed. *What did I expect he was going to say?* "Please don't give up on Brad, Detective Padron," I pleaded. "I need him to be found." My voice broke as I spoke. *I need him to wake me up from this nightmare.*

"Nobody is giving up, Lillian," he said, more compassionately this time.

"Thank you, sir."

"But, Lillian?"

"Yes, Detective?" I held my breath, praying for some encouraging words.

"I hope you understand that some people don't want to be found."

"Yes," I sighed. "That may be true about certain people. But not..."

"You will be among the first to be informed if we get a break. I promise. Now get back to class."

There was a click on the end of the line and he was gone. No condolences, no promises, not even a goodbye. Even the people who were supposed to keep our community safe and bring Brad home were moving on. I hung up the phone and stood to leave, nodding to the waitress as I left.

I started down the sidewalk, trying to decide where to go next since it was too early for me to go home and I definitely wouldn't be returning to school for third period Honor Choir. I heard the faint sound of the diner bell and footsteps behind me and picked up my pace. I suddenly felt afraid. I couldn't decide whether I wanted to run, and I worried that if I tried to my legs wouldn't carry me. *I should have eaten something. Anything.* I realized just how weak I was when a hand grasped my shoulder and my knees trembled beneath me. When I looked up I was met with two piercing blue eyes.

"What are you doing?" I cried, jerking my arm away.

The boy from the diner pulled his hand back and took a deep breath. I searched his face. His eyes were so reminiscent of Brad's that I wanted to look away but felt almost hypnotized.

"I'm sorry I grabbed you. But you forgot your bag." His voice was kind, as it had been that night on the porch of Mandy's house. He extended his other hand, which clutched my backpack I had thoughtlessly left sitting on the stool next to me.

"Oh, thanks. It's okay..."

"Chris," he filled in.

"Chris. Well, thank you, Chris." I took the bag from his hand and gave him a nod. There was an awkward silence that lasted a few moments before I turned to walk away.

"Lillian!" he called out. I stopped in my tracks.

"How do you know my name?" I asked as I turned back towards him.

He suddenly seemed nervous. I saw the motion of his throat as he swallowed. *Has he been watching me? Did he follow me from school?* I looked from left to right to see if anyone else was around. The street was unusually quiet.

"I asked you a question."

"Everyone knows your name," he said, his face turning a pinkish hue. "I mean, because of Brad."

I wrinkled my nose. *Popularity by association. I never dreamed I would benefit from his absence.*

"I'm sorry, that came out wrong," he apologized, shrugging his shoulders.

"It's okay."

He looked at me as he brushed a strand of hair from his eye. "My offer still stands."

"Excuse me?"

"If you want someone to talk to. I can be that someone."

I sighed. "Thanks, but I really don't think…"

"It's still early," he interjected. "But are you interested in joining me for lunch?"

"I'm not hungry," I told him, my eyes drifting to the ground. I knew I needed food, or just a few bites to give me enough fuel to make it home. I had practically been on a three-month hunger strike, unsure if I was fasting in prayer for Brad's return or developing anorexia. My empty stomach rumbled but I hoped he didn't hear it.

"Then we can split something. My treat." He was smiling when I looked up at him.

"Look, I have a boyfriend."

"I know," he said. "I'm not asking you on a date. It's just lunch. Come on, even your eyes look hungry." His smile was sincere.

I glanced around the street to see if anyone from church or school could be watching, but there was no one. I wasn't sure why, but I felt drawn to him—like I *needed* to follow him back into the diner.

"Okay," I finally agreed. *Skipping school, having lunch with a stranger…this isn't me. But who am I becoming? Who am I since Brad disappeared?*

He held the door for me as we returned to the restaurant and we sat down across from each other at a booth with pink, vinyl covered bench seats near the window. The waitress approached us with menus and gave Chris a sly smile.

"She sure is a pretty one," she whispered loudly to him. "Smart boy."

He looked at me and laughed awkwardly once she walked away. I felt guilty for thinking he was cute, but that wasn't the reason I had accepted his lunch invitation. The thought of spending time with someone who didn't get annoyed every time I brought up Brad's name was appealing. I wasn't stupid, it was obvious Anna and the others were tired of hearing me pour over the details of the last time I saw Brad, but I didn't have anyone else to talk to. I wondered if Chris could be a friend who didn't expect me to attend pep rallies and football games as if nothing had changed.

"Order whatever you want," he told me, motioning towards the laminated menu that lay on the table. I didn't need to look. I had been to the diner countless times with my group of friends, and with Brad.

The waitress returned to our table and pulled a pen from the knot of wiry hair on top of her head. "What'll it be, kids?"

"A cheeseburger with onion rings," I replied without glancing at the menu. "And a Coke. Please."

"I'll have the same," he told her with a smile.

We sat in silence for a moment as we waited for our food. Chris tapped his fingers on the metal tabletop.

"So, what's your story?" I blurted out. "Why don't I recognize you from school?"

He laughed as he pulled a napkin from the dispenser and folded it in his hands.

"What's my story, huh? That's a pretty big question before

we even get our drinks."

"Oh, I'm sorry." I grimaced. "I just wondered…"

"Don't apologize. But there's not a lot to tell. Or not a lot worth telling, I should say."

"Good, it won't take long," I said with a small grin. Out of the corner of my eye, I could see Brad's poster hanging on the wall directly behind Chris' head. I looked down at the table for a moment to avoid his ink jet stare.

"Well, first of all, you don't know me from your school because I'm not from here. I just come into town now and then to help out my Grandma."

"If you don't live here, why did you want to come to that first search party for Brad?"

He shrugged. "Seemed like the right thing to do, I guess."

"So, where are you from?" I asked.

"A small town."

"In North Carolina?"

"Yeah. It's just north of Charlotte."

"What's it called?"

"You have to admit," he said with a grin. "For someone who didn't even want me to know her name, you sure do want to know a lot about me."

*There I go again. What is this, twenty questions over burgers and onion rings? Come on Lillian, get it together.* I wasn't ready to explain to him that my social skills were lacking.

"I'm from Gladeville. It's about three hours from here, a one stop light kind of place. Even smaller than Lions Port if you can believe that."

"Are you in school?"

"You could say that."

"What does that mean?" I asked with a shrug.

"I've been homeschooling myself since fifth grade," he said. "My dad's a deadbeat, my mom turned me over to my chain smoking, out of work uncle when I was a kid…and let's just say getting me to school in the morning isn't a top priority."

"Wow, I'm sorry."

"Stop apologizing," he told me. "I'll be all right."

I wasn't sure what else to say. It was suddenly apparent to me that maybe I wasn't the only one on the planet who was hurting. I glanced again to the poster of Brad. Chris noticed my wandering gaze and turned his head to see what had caught my eye.

"Your boyfriend is missing," he said as he looked back at me. "I can't imagine what that feels like."

I couldn't explain what it felt like even if I had wanted to. *It feels like an out-of-body experience. Or a cruel joke. Since Brad has been gone it feels like I am waiting in a long line that never moves.*

"Where do you think he is?" Chris asked.

It was the simplest question, yet I was at a loss for words. "You know," I said. "No one has ever asked me that before."

Chris wrinkled his brow. "Asked where you think Brad is?"

"As if I wasn't an important part of his life," I told him with a nod. "No matter where he is now, it doesn't change the six months we spent together…" My voice trailed off as I spoke the words I had been constantly repeating to myself. They didn't sound any better coming out of my mouth than they did in my head.

"Well, I'm asking you now. Where do you think he is?"

I took a deep breath in and tried to imagine Brad. My mind wandered back to the nightmares of him in the street, yelling at me to leave him alone, and then to the visions of his mangled body hanging from the hook of a crane. These thoughts were all wrong. *Where do I want him to be? Locked in a tower like Cinderella or Sleeping Beauty or one of those princess types? No, that's ridiculous. So where do I think he is? I have absolutely no idea. Where do I want him to be? Here.*

"I look in every ditch, creek bed, dark alley..." I finally said, thinking aloud. "But I don't think he's dead. Maybe he is being held somewhere against his will, or in some sort of trouble. Honestly, I wonder where he is twenty-four hours a day and can never come up with a good answer. But no matter what anyone says or what the statistics point to, I don't believe he ran away. Not from his family. Not from me..."

I was interrupted as the waitress arrived at our table with hot plates brimming with burgers and onion rings. She sat them down in front of us before retrieving our drinks from the counter behind her.

"Eat up, Honeybuns. You won't stay that skinny forever," she chuckled, her voluptuous hips swinging side to side as she walked away.

I reached for my burger with two hands just as she turned around and headed back towards us with her order pad and pencil in hand.

"I'm guessing you two young things should be in school?" she said as she raised her bushy eyebrows.

I cringed and looked to Chris, expecting him to answer. I

wasn't used to breaking the rules.

"But I'm glad you're here," she continued. "Because I need a fresh set of eyes to read this order I scrawled down."

She pushed the notepad in front of my face but all I could make out were light colored scribbles and chicken scratches.

"You know you're getting old when you can't even read your own handwriting!" she said with a laugh. The smell of the burger on the plate hit my nose. My mouth was watering.

"Here, let me take a stab at it," Chris offered. "After years of reading doctor's handwriting for my Mom, I'm kind of a pro." He pulled the paper from her hand and studied it for a moment. "Looks like...two eggs over easy, no salt, and a double order of bacon." He smiled as he handed the pad back to her. "Well that's a little counterproductive, don't you think?"

"That's exactly it! Quite a keeper you have here," she said as she looked to me. "You've heard what they say about a man with good eyes..." She winked and headed back towards the kitchen. I couldn't help but let out a small, uncomfortable laugh.

"Here's to Brad." Chris raised his plastic tumbler of soda. "Here's to Brad being safe." He smiled and I raised my glass to his. As they clanked together I wished everyone could be as optimistic as he was.

Much to my surprise, I devoured my cheeseburger and onion rings in a matter of minutes. I hadn't realized just how hungry I was, both for a hearty meal and someone to talk to. As if someone had put my mouth on fast forward, I raced through the events that had led up to that day. I was very vague when it came to explaining Brad's past and the detective's reaction. It didn't seem fair to Brad to broadcast his private business to yet another stranger.

"Remember, my treat," Chris said as he grabbed the check from the waitress and handed her a twenty-dollar bill.

"Thank you. It was just what I needed."

We sat in silence for a moment and I dabbed the corners of my mouth with a paper napkin, watching him gaze out the window.

"Well, Lillian, it was very nice to officially meet you," he said as he turned back to me and extended a hand.

And just like that, it was over. *Did I say something wrong?* After the conversation we had shared it didn't seem right to simply shake hands, but I placed my hand in his anyway and he gave it a firm tug across the table. His warm grasp around my fingers felt foreign; it had been so long since I'd held Brad's hand.

"I'll be leaving again soon, so I can't say when I will see you again," he told me as he let go. My heart sank.

"Oh…well, thanks for lunch." *I guess this is my cue to leave.* I gathered up my bag and slid out of the bench seat.

"Lillian?"

"Yeah?"

"I…" His eyes searched mine and he opened his mouth again to speak but nothing came out. "I hope I'll see you around," he finally said.

"Me too." I nodded. "See ya."

I sauntered towards the door of the diner, mystified at how suddenly the conversation had ended. Brad's poster stared at me as I turned to exit. *Stop looking at me like that. I did nothing wrong.*

****

I took my time getting home, planning out a slow walk with several detours that would get me to my doorstep at approximately the same time Anna would have been dropping me off. I wandered around the public library, opening and closing hundreds of books without reading a page, before browsing through an over-priced boutique on the town square. It was a few minutes after two o'clock when I started down my driveway. I was surprised to see Anna's blue car parked under the lamppost, she was sitting on my front porch. She stood up when she saw me coming.

"I waited for you after school," she said once I approached.

"Oh, I'm sorry. I had to get out of there…"

"First, I waited by the car," Anna continued. "Then I looked around inside the hallways and in the guidance office. I even checked the bathrooms to make sure you were okay." She crossed her arms and shook her head as she talked.

"I guess I just wasn't thinking…" I sat down on the brick step and she did the same.

"I skipped tennis practice so I could look for you. You couldn't send me a message?"

"My phone died," I told her. "I didn't have any way to reach you."

"Ever heard of the good old-fashioned way? You know, hand write a note and stick it in my locker?"

"I wasn't thinking, okay? I'm really sorry."

"It's fine. Just tell me next time if you don't need a ride."

She let out a sigh. "I was worried about you, I didn't know what had happened."

"I'm sorry, Anna, I should have told you I was leaving…" I wasn't sure how many times I'd have to apologize before she would believe me.

"Okay, well it doesn't matter. The main reason I came over here, " she said, suddenly changing her tone. "Is that me and Thomas were talking about the fall social today! And he told me that Caleb, you've met his friend Caleb Marino, wants to ask you."

"Ask me what?" I said slowly.

"To the dance!"

My jaw dropped open. "What? What did you tell him?"

"Well, I said I thought that would be great! Caleb is such a fun guy…"

"Anna!" I exclaimed. "No…I can't do that. I mean, I don't want to. I can't do that to Brad."

Anna raised her eyebrows and shook her head as if in disbelief. "You can just go as friends, Lil. I didn't mean it had to be like that."

"No. No, I can't, I'm sorry. Can't you guys go with Mandy and Tess?"

"Well, yes, we could…but you know Mandy's dating Parker now, and him and Thomas don't really get along ever since that riff they had last basketball season…" I turned away from her and stared off into the front yard as she continued, attempting to tune her out. "And anyway, I wanted *us* to go. You know, you and me. It's our last fall social before we graduate!"

"I'm not going with Caleb," I snapped. "There's nothing you can say that will change my mind. I already have a boyfriend."

She let out an exasperated sigh. "I know you have a boyfriend, Lil. Thomas knows. Caleb knows. Everyone knows!"

"And what's your point?" I asked.

"My point is that no one, including you, knows where he is!" Her volume rose with every word.

"Anna, come on…"

"When are you going to move on?" she continued. "What if six months from now there is still no sign of him? What about two years? Brad's missing, and it's a terrible feeling not knowing what happened to someone you love. But you could ruin your life waiting on him. If he were here he would tell you to move on…"

"That's not what Brad would tell me. How can you even think that that's what he would tell me? What, have you been rehearsing this?" I asked her, my eyes wide. "In all the time you could have been helping me *find him* you were figuring ways to tell me to *move on*?"

"No! I spent half my summer searching for Brad and you know it! I have scars from the ten thousand mosquito bites I got traipsing through every field in town looking for him! And anyway…oh, forget it." She snapped her head around and looked out across my yard.

"No, go on," I said. "What?"

As she turned back to me I could see the look of anger boiling up in her eyes.

"How much longer do I have to take this!" she shouted.

"What?"

"This! *You*! Do you want to know what people ask me every day? They say, 'how do you keep spending time with Lillian? It's like she's not even there. She's consumed by her own misery'. And I keep defending you and telling people what a hard time you're having…but it's true!"

I opened my mouth to retort but nothing would come out.

"Brad is my friend, too," she went on. "And Thomas's friend. We want to find him just as much as you do, Lillian, whether you believe me or not. We miss him *so much*. But that doesn't mean we are just going to stop *living*…"

"That's not the same. You know it…"

"But it is the same, Lil. It's enough to miss Brad every day but I'm also missing you," she sighed. "You have become a shell of the Lillian that I know."

I looked out across the yard and found myself wishing that Chris were with me.

"I understand that you are hurting. I really do." Anna moved her face in front of mine and tried to catch my eyes. "But you seem to forget those of us who aren't missing, Lil. I'm right here, and I need my best friend. You and Brad were together for six months, but you and me have been friends for over ten years."

"Anna…I'm sorry."

"I'm not asking you to be sorry."

I sat there on the steps, watching her towering over me, numb to her outburst of emotions. She waited for me to say more but my lips remained pursed.

"Where did you go today, anyway?" she asked, changing the subject.

"I just walked into town and got something to eat…I was having a rough morning and then I ran into Chris…" As soon as the words left my mouth I regretted saying it.

"Chris?" she grunted. "Chris who?"

"Chris…" I realized he hadn't told me his last name. "He's just a…friend of mine. I met him at Mandy's Fourth of July party. You don't know him…"

She had stopped listening. "So you're going to sit here and throw a fit when I talk to you about going with our group of friends to the dance, but you're *skipping school* to hang out with some guy you met at a party? Are you listening to yourself?" Anna threw her hands into the air as tears glazed over her eyes.

*She's right, what am I saying?*

"I don't have anything left to say to you," she snapped as she tore off towards her car. "Except, find another ride to school," she yelled without turning around.

I sat there, locked into the brick steps, and didn't try to stop her. There were a million things I wanted to say, a million excuses I wanted to make, but it wouldn't matter. She sped off down the driveway and onto the road, gravel spitting from under her tires as she turned the corner.

I pulled my knees in towards my chest and sat huddled there on the front steps, tugging on the ring around my neck. My friends, my classmates, and even my family were turning against me. Brad's disappearance continued to cut deeper and deeper as I attempted to muddle through my day-to-day life. *If Brad were sitting next to me right now, what would he say to make me feel better? That's a dumb question. If Brad were sitting next to me I wouldn't feel this way.* I put my hands over my face and begged for my prayer to be answered. *Please, Lord. Please help me. Show me what to do.*

My breathing grew heavy and I looked up towards the darkening sky. A cool drop of rain hit my skin and stung like a brisk astringent. It was time to prepare for a storm. *Please bring him home. I can't go on like this much longer.* I heard a distant roar of thunder and suddenly knew what I had to do.

# 8

## lillian white, girl detective

I LAY AWAKE MOST OF THE NIGHT, LISTENING TO the sounds of the storm that had stationed itself above my bedroom. Strong gusts of wind made our old house creek and purr like a kitten. When I closed my eyes I could almost feel the walls around me swaying side to side. I would just get used to the dark when another bolt of lightning lit up the sky, illuminating my room and electrifying Brad's blue eyes on the stack of missing posters that lived on top of my dresser. I was finally drifting off to sleep as the thunder moved into the distance, but it felt like only moments later that the sun began to peek through the clouds and my alarm clock chirped from the nightstand.

I dressed quickly and quietly at 5:45 am, skipping the shower and pulling my dirty hair into a low ponytail. The house was silent, and it needed to stay that way if I was going to get out undetected. I slung my backpack over my shoulder and tiptoed down the hall. My parents had begun stirring behind their closed door so I knew I had to hurry. I scribbled a note to my Mom and set it in front of the coffee pot where she was sure to discover it as soon as she entered the kitchen.

*Walking to school, left early. Be home later. —Lil*

It was a lie, pure and simple, but if I had actually planned to go to school that morning it would have been true, since Anna certainly wouldn't be picking me up. I had been attempting to put off thinking about our conversation and how much my actions seemed to be hurting her. I didn't want to dwell on it. *You're not the only one that's hurting here, Anna.* I might have hurt her, but I refused to let her hurt me. I had to be stronger than that.

I slipped out the side door and started down the driveway. The puddles on the concrete from the overnight downpour were already evaporating in the hot morning sun. There wasn't a car in sight on our narrow road but that would soon change as the morning commute began. I figured as long as I walked in the direction of school no one would suspect anything. I could take the detour from there. *Here goes nothing.*

\*\*\*\*

Six and a half miles and two hours later, I rushed along the gravel road, cursing my parents for never buying me a car and wishing I had at least opted for a bike. Sweat dripped down my forehead and into my eyes but I continued on, dirty and drenched. I heard a sputtering car engine ahead; it grew louder and louder before it died with a loud cough. As I glanced around the open field on either side of me, a brisk chill ran up my spine seeing the gutted skeletons of automobiles scattered across the plain. The freestanding metal structure at the end of the road was becoming closer than I had ever hoped it would be.

This was my last chance to turn back. *Turning back now would mean admitting defeat before I've even tried. He doesn't scare me.* I had obeyed the detective for over three months, and that was more than enough. I slowed my pace as I entered the large doorway of the metal barn and cleared my throat.

"Hello?" I called out. My voice echoed in the vast space.

In front of me, in the center of the building, sat an old hatchback with dust from the dirt floor circling around it. The barn was lit only by the beams of light that jutted through thin slats in the wall, illuminating the particles that danced around me. A thick, musty odor hung in the air.

"Hello!" I cried again.

The engine of the hatchback suddenly revved, and the headlights cut through the darkness in the room. I held my breath and wanted to back away but my feet felt planted in the earthy floor. I continued to stare at the car as the driver's side door opened. I closed my eyes for a split second and hoped it was Brad.

"Hey," a loud voice interrupted my thoughts. "What are you doin' here? Didn't that fat cop tell you to leave me alone?"

He crept towards me, wiping his stained hands on a torn handkerchief. He rubbed the side of his face on his shoulder and I heard the bones in his neck crack. I hoped coming here had not been a mistake.

"Hi, Lizard."

"Answer the question. I said, *what are you doin' here?*"

"You know exactly what I'm doing here," I told him. "I'm looking for Brad."

"Well, I don't see him. Do you?"

"Cut it out, Lizard. I need to talk to you and it's important."

He bit his dirty thumbnail as he stared at me with the same devilish look he had given me that night at graduation.

"Well then step into my office." He took steps toward the door and I followed him cautiously. Once outside the barn he sat down on an old, cloth covered bench that appeared to have come from the inside of a van. Dust rose from the cushion as he settled in. He pulled a pack of cigarettes from his shirt pocket and held it towards me. I shook my head.

"Just tryin' to be polite," he said with a grimacing smile.

"Mm-hmm," I muttered as I sat beside him.

I watched as he slipped a cigarette from the carton and placed it between his lips. He pulled a lighter from inside the pack and inhaled as the flame caught the end of the cigarette. Dozens of butts were scattered on the ground around the bench seat. I truly was in enemy territory.

"Havin' car troubles?" he asked, streams of smoke pouring from his nostrils.

"No."

"Then what brings you all the way out here? You sure

never made the trek before." Lizard looked me up and down, sucking the life out of his glowing stick.

"It's about Brad." I turned away and peered out into the field. The rusty frame of what had once been a school bus stared back at me.

"What about him?" Lizard tossed the cigarette to the ground and stomped with his large black boot. He gave me his usual cold stare, but I thought I could see a sadness in his eyes.

"I just need to know…do you have any information that might help me find him? *Anything at all?* You're his best friend." My voice sounded weak and broken. *I remember how strong I used to be.*

It was Lizard's turn to turn away. He leaned forward, digging his elbows into his knees. "That punk is no friend of mine," he said coldly.

"What are you talking about?"

"Well, you should know better than anybody, shouldn't ya? You stuck your meat hooks in him and got him thinkin' he was better than everybody else since he was datin' a church girl."

"That's not true! How can you even say that." I bit down on the skin on the sides of my mouth. *You need him on your side. Don't say anything stupid.* "Look, Lizard, whatever kind of resentment you're harboring towards Brad and I, it has to stop. Okay? *Our* best friend is missing and we may be the only ones who can find him."

"If you're so smart why haven't you found him already, huh? What, you couldn't *pray* him back?" He cleared his throat and hawked a glob of spit onto the ground a few feet in front of me.

"Trust me, you're the last person in the world I wanted to ask for help," I told him. "Why do you think I waited all this time? Look, I wouldn't be here if I had any other options. You can hang up on me, threaten me, report me, change your number, whatever. But I can't take this anymore. I have to find him." Anyone with half a soul could have recognized the heartbreak in my eyes. "So, please…is there *anything* you haven't told me?"

I ran my fingers through my ponytail as I thought of Brad and Lizard sitting on this same bench. *Maybe they sat here and smoked cigarettes together, discussing life. Or maybe this is where they planned their crimes, drawing a getaway map in the dirt.*

"A man came lookin' for Brad," Lizard finally said.

"What do you mean? When?" I sputtered. "Recently?"

"The day before he…the day before graduation."

"What?" I cried. "Who was it?"

"Look, I didn't recognize the guy. He said he needed to talk to Brad, and I told him he wasn't here." Lizard shrugged his shoulders and pulled another cigarette from the carton.

"Did he say anything else?"

"Nope."

"Did *you* say anything else?"

"I just told him where he might find him." He exhaled and a cloud of smoke drifted towards my face.

"As in…where?" I asked, afraid to hear his answer to my question. "Did you tell him where he lived?"

Lizard slowly inhaled on the cigarette again. "Yeah," he coughed.

"Lizard, who was it?" I demanded.

"Some old guy. Never seen him before then and ain't seen him since."

"What did he look like?"

"He looked the way old guys look!" he raised his voice. "Grey hair, fat, *old*. I told you, I ain't seen him since then."

I threw my hands in the air. "So, some guy just randomly showed up here, and you told him where Brad lived? *The day before he went missing?* Please tell me you told the police." I felt a rush of emotions coming over me, an overwhelming mix of excitement and anger. My fingers were trembling. *Did Lizard sell Brad up the river by giving this stranger his address? Or is this the clue we have been missing this whole time?*

"I tried to tell Brad after graduation. You should remember it quite well…" he said with a grunt. "He brushed me off. *Because of you.*"

"That's not what I asked you. Did you tell the police?"

Lizard didn't answer me. He stood up and finished his smoke as he walked into the grass.

"Lizard…" I continued, moving towards him. "*Did you tell the police?*" I already knew the answer.

"Look, Lillian. The business I run here ain't exactly legit. I couldn't have the cops crawlin' over this place. If they had started askin' questions about where I got some of my equipment they probably would've tried to shut me down…" The cold gaze returned to his eyes and the sympathy for his friend disappeared.

"You selfish pig."

"Oh, gimme a break. You really do think you're so much better than me. Like you wouldn't have done the same." He raised his voice and I walked towards him. I brought my face close to his and held back the urge to slap him.

"See, that's where I *am* better than you. I would give everything I have if it meant finding Brad. If something has happened to him because you lied to the police to protect yourself…" I started to back away when he grabbed my forearm and yanked my body towards his.

"I jus' told you, I didn't tell the police for a reason. So you best keep your mouth shut." He peered down his nose at me and I could feel his breath on my face.

"I'm not afraid of you," I said as I jerked my arm away from his grasp. "And Brad wasn't either. That's why you're so ticked off! He was tired of playing your stupid head games and doing your dirty work." I knew I should stop, but I felt words growing in my mouth, ready to jump off of my tongue. "And if you ever needed any further affirmation of why Brad chose me over you, I think you just got your answer."

I turned and started off down the road. Lizard didn't follow or call out to me, but I hadn't expected him to. I glanced behind me to see him walking back into the garage without another word. As I picked up my pace and began running I heard the sputtering car engine behind me. *If someone came looking for Brad, a man Lizard had never seen, what does it mean? What will happen when I tell the police? Will this change the whole course of the investigation?*

Once I was far enough away, I slowed my steps to even my breathing. I pulled my phone from my back pocket and held it above my head in search of a signal. Nothing. I knew I could head farther into town and try the call again…or I could go directly to the police station with the information. It was a little after eleven o'clock in the morning and I knew if I got there close enough to lunchtime there would be much less suspicion about my arrival during the middle of a school day.

I wanted to see the expression on Detective Padron's face when I told him. *I want to look him in the eye and remind him why he needs to be looking for Brad. I want to remind him that Brad didn't run away…and this tip proves it. Or at least suggests it…or it's a mere coincidence….* I shook away the doubt. The news from Lizard was all I had left at this point. I had a new spring in my step—like I had been given a tiny sliver of hope. *Please Lord, let this be it.*

****

I had only visited the police station twice in my life and only once during the investigation. When I was thirteen I went to the precinct to report my cat Gracie missing. The woman at the desk had smiled and handed me an old Lost Dog flyer to use as an example so I could create some of my own. Two days later Gracie showed up on our back porch, fat, happy, and pregnant. I had turned my neighborhood upside down over the course of those forty-eight hours looking for her. I never imagined that four years later I would be searching for the boy who had teased me when I knocked on his door and asked if he had seen her.

The next time I climbed the stone steps to the station was exactly two weeks to the day after Brad had vanished. I was frantic and desperate and had made a scene in the lobby, crying and demanding that I speak with Detective Padron. He had called my parents and recommended I seek psychiatric help during this 'transitional time' but Mom chalked it up to PMS and told me to pull it together. I had been too embarrassed and ashamed to return since then, but I had to put my pride aside. Anyway, I was done caring what everyone thought, and it was written all over my makeup-less face.

"Hello," I said to the receptionist as I heard the heavy door close behind me. "Can I please speak with Detective Padron?"

I could tell by the wide-eyed look on her face she recognized me from my outburst.

"Is there a problem or emergency?" she asked delicately, her hand reaching for the phone at her desk.

"No ma'am. But I have new information in the Brad Lee Missing Person's Case. I'm Lillian White."

"I see." She nodded and mumbled something into the phone after dialing an extension. I hoped it was Detective Padron's and not Security.

"Mm-hmm. Yes." She looked up at me as she spoke. "He will see you in his office." She extended her arm and motioned down a hallway made up of cubicle walls. "Last door on the left, his name is on the glass."

I thanked her and made my way past cluttered desks and ringing telephones in a room that reeked of burnt coffee and cigarette smoke. A few police officers poured over stacks of paperwork, they each nodded to me as I walked by. There was no reason to be on high alert in a sleepy town like Lions Port.

I had barely tapped on the frosted glass door that lead to Detective Padron's office when a deep voice called out, "Come in."

I turned the brass knob and pushed open the door to see

him seated behind an oversized wooden desk, sipping from a colorful coffee mug. A large family portrait hung on the wall behind the desk next to his diploma. In the photo, Detective Padron was smiling on the beach with his arms around his blonde wife and two young blonde daughters. I had never pictured him with a family, let alone a pretty trophy wife and kids cute enough to have been cut out of a magazine. I couldn't decide if I should let down my guard or be even more intimidated than usual.

"Is this going to be a daily thing now, Lillian?" he asked with a closed-mouth smile as he motioned for me to sit in one of the chairs in front of his desk.

"I don't know," I said as I slid onto the sticky leather. "I mean, no. Or, well, I guess it just depends." *Get it together. You're rambling on like an idiot.*

"So, what have you got for me?" he asked, leaning onto his elbows.

"I have information that an older man was asking around about where to find Brad on the day *before* he disappeared."

"Okay." He nodded. "Who's your source?"

"Well, it's…" There was no hiding that I had gone against the detective's orders. I hoped he wouldn't remember telling me not to contact him. "It was Michael Lizardo. The man came by his shop on Thursday, May fifteenth and Lizard gave him Brad's address. He told him where he lived!"

Detective Padron didn't immediately jump out of his seat as I had expected him to; in fact, I wasn't sure if I even saw him blink.

"You spoke to Mr. Lizardo?"

*Busted.* "Well, yes. I sort of ran into him…" I lied.

"Did he describe the man?"

"Grey hair, overweight…Lizard said he was an older guy."

"Well, you've just described half the officers in our precinct," he replied with a grunt. "That's not going to get us very far."

"I tried to get a better one but…"

"Did he give you a description of the vehicle he was driving," he interrupted. "Or a license plate number?"

"Um, no…I don't know if he has that…"

"What was his name?"

"I don't know…Lizard said he didn't know who he was."

"And you never actually saw this man with Brad? Can Mr. Lizardo place the man at the graduation ceremony?"

*If I say 'I don't know' one more time he is probably going to throw me out of this office. I could lie and say that he did see him at graduation and that he was watching Brad…but where would that get us?*

"Lizard didn't really want to talk to me," I finally admitted. "And he doesn't want to talk to the police either, that's why he didn't tell you about this man when you initially questioned him. But that just means he's hiding something! I think if you go to him…"

"I'll give him a call." Detective Padron leaned back in his chair with his elbows out, resting his head in the palms of his hands. "But without any more information, I hope you can see that this doesn't really give me anything to work with. I can't exactly put out a BOLO for a non-descript, fat old man who may or may not have wanted to speak with Brad the day before he went missing. And no one reported seeing anything suspicious at the Lee household that night so we have no reason to believe this man got Brad's address and waited for him outside his home."

"But what if he intercepted Brad before he ever got home…maybe on that stretch of road right past my house that is enclosed by trees on either side…"

"That area was thoroughly searched and there was no evidence of a struggle. If someone stopped Brad on the way home that night he could have gotten willingly into the car with them."

"No…he wouldn't have…" *Wouldn't have what? Accepted a ride from a stranger? I am losing this fight.*

"If the man knew to come to Mr. Lizardo's shop to look for Brad, it sounds like he wasn't a stranger," he said, reading my mind. "And with the dealings Brad had made in the past, it's not unlikely that this man came looking for…"

*Don't say it.* "Brad doesn't deal drugs."

The detective let out a sigh and once again leaned forward onto his elbows on the desk. "As I said, I'll talk to Mr. Lizardo." He looked down his nose at me and changed his tone to a more delicate sound. "But please understand that this information isn't necessarily going to change anything in Brad's case. Kids nowadays see episodes of CSI: Atlanta and that Law and Whatever show and think law enforcement should be super human like those hokey cops on TV. That's just not the case."

I cringed at the word *kids*. He wasn't taking me seriously. I decided to make a last ditch effort and try another approach—one I had seen those 'hokey TV cops' fall for many times.

"Are those your kids, Detective Padron?" I motioned to the picture hanging behind his head.

"Those are my girls." He nodded without looking back. "Julie and Becca, they are six and nine."

"And what would you do if they were missing?" I asked, leaning forward onto the desk to match his stature.

"Well," he paused. "I don't know what I would do if they were missing. Because, as I'm sure you can assume, they are not. But I do know I'll be running background checks on any prospective boyfriends that come calling, so they aren't running around town with juvenile delinquents."

*Is this aimed at me? Or is he taking a jab at my parents for not protecting me from Brad and his haunted past? Either way, my approach didn't work. I'm defeated.* I didn't dare cause a scene as I had months ago, it hadn't helped then and it certainly wasn't going to make a difference now. I pushed the chair I was sitting in away from the desk, the legs squealed across the tile floor as it moved.

"I'm sorry if you think I've wasted your time," I told him as I headed towards the door.

"You haven't wasted my time, Lillian." I turned to see him shaking his head. I detected a sympathetic look in his eyes I'd never noticed before. "I just hate to see you wasting yours. Now get back to school." The corners of his mouth turned up in a small, sad smile.

All I could do was nod. I left the room, pulling the door closed gently behind me. I felt a tickle in my sinuses and opened my eyes wide trying to dry the oncoming flow of tears.

*Why does it always come down to his past? If Brad were an honor student with a full ride to Yale I bet they would be looking for him. They would look harder for him if he had escaped from prison than they are now! He's not good enough to matter, and not bad enough to count. And why does everyone think that it's their place to tell me I'm wasting my time by continuing to care about Brad? What is so wrong with loving someone in spite of their past?*

# 9

## the honest truth

I PUSHED OPEN THE DOORS TO THE POLICE station and was blinded by the bright sun as I rushed down the stone steps. *Please Lord, don't let me cry here. Please let me make it somewhere, anywhere but here.* I blinked the sunspots away from my eyes and saw a tall male figure on the sidewalk coming towards me.

"Lillian!"

*Brad?* I stopped in my tracks, trying to focus on him.

"Hey! I was hoping I would find you here."

I recognized his dark hair first and realized it was Chris. But I didn't get the sudden sinking feeling I usually got when I discovered it wasn't Brad. Instead, I wanted to run to him and hug him as tears continued to well up in my eyes.

"Hi. I thought you were leaving…what are you doing here?" I felt a tear rolling down my face before my hand could wipe it away.

"Hey. Hey, it's okay." Chris put his hand on my shoulder as I lowered my head to hide the reddening of my cheeks. "Come on, let's take a walk."

Chris' hand drifted onto to my back as we started down the sidewalk, his fingers rubbing back and forth against my sweaty t-shirt. Just like a young child needs their parents to hold them and tell them everything is all right when they cry, I felt like I needed his touch.

"What happened in there?" he asked once my breathing had calmed.

"Nothing," I sighed, staring at my feet as we walked. "Nothing happened. That's the whole problem."

He suddenly stopped in his tracks and pulled his hand away from my back.

"Do you need to get back to school?"

"No. Not today." *Maybe not ever.*

"Well, then let's get out of here."

"What?" I jerked my head towards him and searched his face. *Is he asking me to run away with him?*

"I mean, let's get off this busy street," he responded with a laugh. "I don't want someone to see you."

"Oh, right." *If he had asked me to run away with him, what would I have said?*

"What did you think I meant?" He smiled.

I shrugged my shoulders. *What am I supposed to say? I'm*

*starved for male attention…or any normal attention for that matter…and I'd go anywhere you asked me to? That definitely wouldn't come out right.*

"Is there anywhere we can go?" Chris asked.

"Yes, I know the perfect place."

I shouldn't have said it. *I knew I shouldn't say it before I even opened my mouth but I said it anyway. It is wrong on so many levels.* But I couldn't stop myself. Before I could re-think my decision, I was leading Chris to the lake. I was asking him to follow me to a place I hadn't been since the search party three days after Brad disappeared. I was leading him to sacred ground.

****

"Well, this is it," I said quietly as we approached the waters edge.

"This place is incredible. I had no idea this town had something this cool." Chris knelt to the ground and dipped his fingers into the clear water.

"This is where we had our last date. The night…" I drifted off.

"Oh, wow." He stood up and looked into my eyes. "I'm sorry. You didn't have to bring me here if…"

"No," I cut him off. "It's good. I wanted to. I needed to come here."

I looked around the park. Over the course of the summer, nothing had changed. The grass was still green and lush, the lake water was still sparkling, and the trees were still dancing to the rhythm of the breeze.

"I have to admit, I came to town today to find you," Chris said as he lowered himself onto the ground.

"You did?" I asked, sitting down a few inches away from

him.

"Yeah. I…I guess I've just been thinking a lot."

I searched his eyes. "About what?"

"Well, without sounding like a total creep…" he cleared this throat. "I've been thinking about you." I looked at him with a puzzled expression. There was a look in his blue eyes I hadn't noticed before. "I needed to get something off my chest."

"Chris…" I wasn't sure what to say.

"I haven't been completely honest with you."

My heart dropped. "Wait…what are you talking about?"

He suddenly seemed nervous and glanced over his shoulder.

"All right, seriously, Chris," I said. "What's going on?"

"Sorry." He snapped his head back towards me. "I thought I heard something."

I glanced behind us in the direction he had been looking, expecting to see a dog walker or someone out for a jog. But there was no one. We were alone. *I'm alone with someone who is practically a complete stranger. No one knows I'm here, no one knows who he is, and if he has been lying to me then I might not even know who he is.* I squeezed Brad's ring in my fist.

"I just needed to tell you," he started to speak but hesitated. "Yesterday, when we were talking at lunch, there's something I should have said." He wouldn't look at me when he spoke, he stared out across the lake and watched as a small fish jumped above the water line.

I wrinkled my brow. "What do you mean?"

"I was there that day," he finally said. He still wasn't making eye contact.

"What day?" I asked, my heart rate increasing. "The day Brad…"

"No," he stopped me. "Not the day he went missing. Two days later."

I tried to think back to the early days of Brad's disappearance, but they were all a blur.

"Chris, please just tell me what you're saying," I insisted. "I don't understand what you're trying to tell me." I tugged on his shoulder, turning him to face me.

"I saw you that Sunday," he said with a sigh. "You were walking down your street and something scared you. That something was me."

"Wait…" The memories of that afternoon came flooding back to me. "The noise I heard in the trees, that was you?"

He nodded.

"Why didn't you say anything when I called out?"

"I wanted to," he told me. "But I didn't know what to say."

"Well, what were you doing there? Have you been watching me?" I asked. "Is that what this is about?"

"No." Chris shook his head. "Nothing like that. I was just looking around and…"

"And what?"

"And then I saw you," he said. "I saw the expression on your face. You seemed so…so hurt."

I started to speak, but no words formed in my mouth. *He's right. I am hurt.*

"Anyway," Chris continued. "I wanted to meet you. So that's why I was at that party last month…and at the diner yesterday. Because of you."

"So you *have* been watching me."

"It sounds bad when you say it like that," he said sheepishly. "But yes."

I shrugged. "So why are you telling me this now?"

"Because." Chris let out a sigh. "Because I've lost someone, too. And I understand what it's like to not have any answers and feel like you've been betrayed."

I started to tell him that no one understands, and he couldn't possibly know what it was like. But I stopped myself.

"We don't deserve to be hurt by the ones we love." He stared at me, searching my face, and the words resonated.

"You're right," I whispered, trying to overcome the lump in the back of my throat. "We don't."

This cute, blue-eyed stranger had once again found the right words to say. *We don't deserve to be hurt by the ones we love. But who are 'we'? He and I? Brad? Or was I the one hurting people? Like Anna.*

"I guess the truth is that you and I are a lot alike." Chris' eyes locked with mine, drawing me in. My heart rate increased. "I don't like to tell people about what I've gone through with my family," he continued, holding his gaze. "But you...it's like you get me more than anyone else ever has because you understand what it's like to be hurt. Or to be lost...I can't really explain it."

"I know what you mean," I said, nodding. I wanted to admit I had been thinking about him, too. "You don't feel so alone when you know someone else is struggling just as much as you are."

"Exactly."

Suddenly, we were sharing a moment. We sat frozen for several seconds, staring into each other's eyes, before he started leaning towards me. I held my breath as he reached up and gently touched the side of my face with his hand. His fingertips were soft and hot against my skin. As I let myself move closer to him, I shut my eyes and my mind started to drift back to that night at the lake, sitting in the very same spot with Brad.

*Brad. What am I doing?*

"I can't." I pulled away, shaking my head. I could barely catch my breath. "Chris, I'm so sorry."

He dropped his head. "Don't apologize, it's okay. I'm sorry, too. I shouldn't have…"

"I think you're wonderful," I whispered. "I really do. And I have enjoyed every moment with you over the past few days. But I can't do this to Brad. It's not right." I looked down at my hands—they were shaking.

"I understand," he said. "Don't worry about it. It's my fault."

I tried to shake away the curious thought of what it would be like to kiss Chris, insisting I didn't have feelings for him like that. I wasn't sure if it was a lie or not, but I couldn't let myself believe I could have feelings for anyone other than Brad.

"Lillian, can I ask you something?" he said after a moment.

"Of course."

"How long…" Chris cleared his throat. "How long are you going to keep waiting for him?"

I was taken aback. "What? What do you mean?"

"He doesn't deserve you."

"How can you say that?" I exclaimed as I jumped to my feet. "You don't even know him."

"I don't have to know him. I can see what he is putting you through, Lil!" He rose to stand next to me, motioning with his hands as he spoke.

"Stop it."

"I'm only trying to help you."

"So was this your plan the whole time?" Tears welled up in my eyes again. "Pretend you understand what I'm going through so you can make a move?"

"What?" Chris shook his head. "No, of course not. Lillian, just listen, please." He gently grabbed my elbow and pulled me in close to him as a tear rolled down my left cheek. He wiped it away with his thumb. "Hey, it's okay."

I looked up at him through my wet lashes. "Please don't tell me to move on, Chris. *Everyone* tells me to move on. I can't take it from you, too."

"I know. I'm sorry. It came out wrong."

I pulled myself out of his grasp and crossed my arms close to my body. "So then, how did you mean for it to come out?"

He motioned me towards the ground and we sat side by side on the plush grass.

"What I wanted to say is that…I spent a long time falling into a depression because of things that happened with my family. I wanted things to go back to how they used to be. But one day I realized that no matter what happened, my life would *never* be the way it was before. Too much damage had already been done." Chris put his hand on my knee and squeezed.

"You never have to stop loving Brad, but please don't let this break you."

*Too late. I'm already broken.*

"I just want him here," I told him as I wiped my tears. "I need answers. I need to find out where he is."

"I know."

"And I want him to explain why he kept so many things from me..." I went on. "I want to know who the man is who came looking for him the night before graduation!" I let out a groan.

Chris cocked his head. "A man?"

"Yes. He came to Lizard's the night before Brad disappeared. That's why I went to the police today, to tell them, but they aren't going to do anything."

"Do you know what he looked like?"

"Old, fat, gray hair." I shrugged. "Apparently the description of half the cops in the precinct, according to Detective Padron. But Lizard gave him Brad's address. He told him where he could to find him. The detective said it might not be related. I don't see how it *couldn't* be related. A strange man shows up the *night before* Brad disappears...I mean, what do you think?"

"I..." Chris looked at me, his mouth open. "I don't know. I'm sorry, Lillian."

"Yeah," I said with a sigh. "I don't know either."

Chris suddenly sprung to his feet. "I should go."

"What? Really?"

"I'm sorry, I didn't realize how late it had gotten. I have to get back to Gladeville by tonight."

"Oh." My heart dropped. "When will you be back?"

"I'm not sure. But I'll see you soon." He smiled. "Can I walk you into town?"

I shook my head. "That's okay, I'm going to hang here for a little longer."

"Alright. Be careful." He extended his arms and wrapped them around my back in a tight hug. I inhaled as I squeezed his neck, he smelled sweet. "Please think about what I said," he whispered as he held me for a moment longer.

"I will."

Once we separated, Chris reached into his back pocket and pulled out a tired, paperbound book and placed it in my hands. The cover was so badly faded that I couldn't make out the title.

"What is this?" I asked, flipping through the pages.

"It's about coping with grief. I found it in a used bookstore years ago. I don't know if it will help you, but I wanted you to have it." As he spoke he adjusted the satchel over his shoulder. "I've found that sometimes it helps to mourn someone, even if they haven't died."

"Thank you, Chris," I said as I took the book from his hand. "Really."

"Are you going to be okay here?"

I nodded. I couldn't explain why, but wanted him to reach out to me again. He gave me a smile that lifted up one side of his lip as I stood there with my arms stiff by my side, wondering how and why he always seemed to come in and out of my life so quickly. *To disappear...*

"Goodbye, Lillian. I'm sorry."

I didn't know what he was apologizing for. I nodded and

forced a smile, sharing one last look with him before he rushed up the grassy knoll. He vanished from my sight as he ran up the wooded path that had led us to the clearing. I clutched his book in my hands and felt overcome with sadness. He, too, was gone.

# 10

## dead girl walking

THE HOUSE WAS QUIET WHEN I GOT HOME. I figured my mom would be arriving shortly with Graham and Eliza in tow and my dad would follow soon after. I wanted to take advantage of what little solitude I had. After taking a long, hot shower, I spent the rest of the afternoon in my room with the contents of Brads and my memory box strewn across the floor as I had done a dozen times before. I was attempting to piece together a puzzle—as if our entire relationship had been a game of Clue and I was collecting the facts. But I didn't believe that old movie ticket stubs and notes folded into origami were clues to Brad's whereabouts.

I had seen countless cases of missing teenagers in made-for-TV movies, and in every case there were obvious hints. Sometimes anonymous letters arrived in the mail, each with a single word that revealed the missing's location once they were all pieced together, or newspaper clippings with random sentences underlined that created a ransom note. But I hadn't received any mysterious phone calls, no notes had arrived with magazine cut outs, and no matter how many times Brad had taken me to the double feature at the Moonlight Drive-in Theatre, I wasn't convinced that he was trying to tell me something through a string of movie titles.

The only thing in the box that seemed to be of more significance now that he was missing was a handwritten note he had jotted on the back of a ripped piece of Chemistry homework.

*Thank you for seeing me for who I am and not who I was.*

He ended it with a doodled smiley face and his initials. When I originally found it in my locker it made me giggle and I had carried it with me the rest of the week. I didn't ask him 'who he was' because, at the time, it wasn't important. Who he was before me was someone who wasn't with me. That was that. Plain and simple. I didn't want to hear about any of his previous relationships and he didn't need to learn about the two tragic weeks I spent attempting to date Glee Club President, Logan Swanson.

I heard a door slam and knew my quiet time had ended all too soon. Footsteps moved quickly down the hall towards my room and after a brisk knock I turned to see my mother standing in my doorway, her arms crossed tightly against her chest.

"Where were you today?" she asked, her tone stern.

"What do you mean?" I said cautiously as I stood. *Don't give up too much information yet. What does she know?*

"I mean exactly what I said. Where were you today?"

"Mom, I was at school…" I pieced my lie together slowly. I would rather have her stop me sooner than later once she called my bluff.

"Lillian, do not lie to me." *Busted.*

"I…I…" I knew it was no use. I looked down at the floor and let out a sigh mixed with a deep groan.

"Principal Carver called me at the store to ask if you were all right. I find out not only have you not set foot inside the school doors today, you ran out of your class yesterday and didn't go back. What is going on with you?" She uncrossed her arms, throwing her hands up in the air.

"Look, Mom, I'm sorry I skipped class, but it's just…it's just too hard to be back there," I insisted. "I can't go anywhere in that school without being reminded of Brad. You've got to put yourself in my shoes and try to understand what I'm going through."

"Lillian, you've known going back to school was going to be hard. But going back is *not* an option so you need to figure out how to deal with it."

"But, Mom…" My voice broke in a tired whine.

"You only get one shot at your senior year. If you screw up your graduation by slacking off and skipping class you will regret it for the rest of your life."

"I get it. I just…"

"Every college you apply to is going to be looking at your GPA and attendance record. I cannot stress to you how important it is that you…"

"I don't want to talk about college right now, Mom." I walked across the floor and plopped down onto my bed in hopes she would let it go. But she followed me into the room and continued to speak as she stood above me.

"Well, it needs to be talked about, Lillian. You need to start focusing on applications and essays. You've let the entire summer go by without so much as a college tour. And if you had any hopes of being awarded a vocal scholarship…"

"I know all this, Mom. But I don't want to talk about it now and I don't want to talk about it later. I'm not going to college next year." I leaned back onto my headboard and picked at a pulled thread in my comforter. My mother's face went blank.

"What are you talking about?" she asked. "Why would you not go to school next year?"

I shrugged my shoulders. "I'm just not going. I made up my mind."

I wasn't sure *when* I had made up my mind. Maybe I had decided right at that moment or maybe my mind had been made up since the day Brad disappeared, but I knew I couldn't do it. Not yet.

"You made up your mind?" she repeated with a scoff as she sat down next to me on my bed.

I nodded in response, noticing the visible anger in her eyes.

"You haven't worked as hard as you did so you could blow

off your education for a boy," she told me, shaking her head as she folded her hands on her lap. "I know this has something to do with Brad, Lillian."

"Of course it has something to do with Brad, Mom. *Everything* has to do with Brad, why can't you get that!" I snapped. I could feel tears building up in my eyes and tried to blink them away.

"Lillian, Brad has been gone for months now and you are the only one who can't seem to move on with your life. I don't understand why you would change your mind about going to school because of him. You can't throw your future away…"

The lump in my throat made it hard to speak, but I forced out the words. "But what if he is found and comes back…and I'm gone? Like he doesn't matter to me at all?"

I had never said it out loud before. My mom sat there beside me on the bed silently for a moment. Her shoulders rose and fell as she took a deep breath.

"And what if he doesn't come back?"

I turned to her with a look of shock but her eyes had grown cold and unfeeling. I was losing the battle. And as much as I hated to admit it, I knew it was a fair question.

"You're grounded for the rest of the week." Her empty eyes locked onto mine. "I will drive you to school and you *will* go to class, every single one, and come straight home afterward. You need to think long and hard about what your future looks like, with or without Brad in it."

Mom stood up and left the room, pulling the door closed behind her before I could retort. I wasn't mad, and I wasn't surprised at how she had reacted. I was numb. Chris' words echoed again in my mind. *We don't deserve to be hurt by the ones we love.* He wasn't talking about just him and me. He was talking about everyone around us. I was hurting my parents. I was hurting Anna. And I was hurting myself. None of us deserved this.

I knew my mom was right. I rubbed Brad's class ring between my thumb and forefinger. *Why am I putting my life on hold and waiting for Brad to be found after he lied to me about his past? Am I being a complete fool for thinking that I could have any kind of future with him even when he is found?* I couldn't think about it. And I couldn't make any decisions until I had answers.

I fell back onto my bed and wriggled my way under the covers, pulling them up to my chin and letting my tears wet the edge of the comforter. I pinched my eyes shut. *What am I supposed to do? What am I supposed to do if I can't let go and I can't move on? How am I supposed to go on living like this? If there is a chance I will spend the rest of my life not knowing what happened to him, will I ever be normal again? Please don't let that happen. Don't keep him away from me any longer. Please, Lord, bring him home. Please just help me cope.*

Then I remembered the book from Chris. I picked it up off of my nightstand and thumbed through the worn pages. Inside the front cover was his name and address, written lightly in pencil.

"Chris Colvin," I whispered to myself. It was a nice name; it rolled easily off my tongue. *Someone as nice as Chris should have a nice name.*

I opened to the first chapter. *What your loss means to you.* I attempted to read the first few sentences but my mind wandered. *What does my loss mean to me? Who is the one who is really lost?* Lately, I had started to feel like I was even farther gone than Brad. I was the one in the Lions Port wormhole screaming for help but no one could hear me. *It's as if Brad took me with him. And wherever we are, I can't find my way home.*

I didn't want to keep hurting people just as much as I didn't want to keep hurting. Flipping through more pages, I searched for highlighted passages, dog-eared corners, or any sort of messages from Chris, but there were none. I closed the book with a sigh and laid it back on my nightstand. *I'm not ready to mourn Brad. My loss means everything to me.*

****

I spent the next two weeks walking the halls of school like a ghost. I was there, I studied, my grades were decent and my attendance was flawless, but I wasn't really *there*. It was as if I had shut myself off. The short rides to and from school were mostly silent, apart from Graham and Eliza bickering in the back seat. My parents hadn't brought up the C word again, but I was waiting for the day. I decided I wasn't going to fight them, and whether it meant enrolling in the local community college or moving halfway across the world, I would just do it. I was so tired of being a disappointment to my friends and family.

Anna and I still hadn't spoken since the argument on my front porch. I figured she was waiting for me to apologize but I couldn't bring myself to do it, not yet. I had caught her looking at me several times when we passed each other in the school halls but she always turned away when her eyes caught mine. After my brief grounding ended, Mom suggested I call

Anna and ask her to pick me up for school the following Monday, but I made up a story about her class schedule and requested my mom continue to drive me for the remainder of the semester. I could have walked but I didn't have the energy, and I knew it wasn't the right time to have the 'when do I get my own car' conversation.

The heat hadn't let up much even as the days rolled into mid-September, yet Brad's case remained as frigid as an icebox. Detective Padron claimed he had interviewed Lizard again and was following up on the new lead, but I saw no changes in the case and heard no breaking newscasts or announcements of suspects in Brad's disappearance. If 'following up' meant scribbling the information in Brad's case file and shoving it back up on the shelf, then I supposed maybe he was telling the truth. But it didn't seem fair. *Nothing seems fair anymore.*

I kept my eyes peeled for Chris every time I went into town, but there was no sign of him. I found myself constantly thinking back to our exchange at the lake and wondered if he was choosing to stay away from me. He had his own problems, after all, and probably didn't need the stress of a needy, emotionally unavailable friend. I didn't feel like I had known him long enough to miss him, but I wanted to see him again. I wanted to look into his blue eyes. *I want to see him because he reminds me of Brad. I want to see Brad.*

****

Four months and three days after Brad's graduation, there was finally a break in the case, but it was one none of us were prepared for. I was sitting attentively at a second-row desk in my fourth period AP English class when there was a sudden frantic pounding on the door. Mrs. Cranson stopped her lecture mid-sentence and rushed towards the sound as my classmates glanced around the room at each other. The door swung open, revealing Anna. Her eyes were wild and her right hand was clenched in a fist as if she were still knocking.

"I need to talk to Lillian White," she said. "It's an emergency."

Mrs. Cranson looked confused and unsure of what to do, but she nodded and looked back at me as she motioned to Anna. *When everyone knows that your boyfriend has been missing for four months, hall passes don't really apply.* I closed the book on my desk and grabbed for my small cloth bag from the rack under my seat, assuming it was a mere tampon emergency. *She'll have to apologize now. I'm her last resort.*

"I'll be right back," I whispered to Mrs. Cranson as I followed Anna into the hall. She was wringing her hands and chewing on the edge of her bottom lip as her eyes searched mine.

"What's up?" I asked nonchalantly once the classroom door closed behind us. We were alone in the long, dim hallway.

"They found a body," she spurted out.

My heart stopped. I suddenly felt as if a sack of bricks had been whacked across my chest.

"Wait, what?" I thought I must be the victim of a cruel joke. My friendship with Anna was beyond repair if she thought she could make me the butt of a game of truth or dare.

"They found..." Anna fought back tears. "A body. Of an adult male."

I studied her face. Her eyes were moist. I found myself

wanting to believe that my best friend of ten years *would* be so hateful as to make up a gruesome story because that was the easier answer.

"Anna, what are you saying?" I asked. "Are you telling me the truth? I swear, if you're making this up…" *Please be making this up. Please be making this up.*

"Lil! No, of course not." She shook her head. "I'm so sorry…it's true."

I could tell she wanted to reach out to me but was reminded that we hadn't been on the best of terms. In fact, it was the first time in the decade we had been friends that we hadn't spoken for more than a few days.

"Where did you hear this?" The halls were still quiet. This was information that obviously hadn't gotten around school yet.

"Mrs. Lee was having lunch with my mom when she got a phone call. Mom said Mrs. Lee was going down to the police station to talk with the detective…"

It was becoming real. I felt sick to my stomach, the chicken sandwich I had eaten for lunch suddenly seemed to be caught my throat.

"I have to get out of here." I looked to Anna, my face was desperate. She nodded.

"I'll talk to Mrs. Cranson." She fished around in her purse and pulled out her bedazzled key ring. "Go get in my car, I'll meet you there."

I couldn't speak; I just tore off down the hallway, shuffling my feet under me as I walked because I didn't have the energy to run. Brad's ring around my neck bounced sharply against my check as I moved. My mind raced. There were so many things I didn't know. *Where was he found? Is the body recognizable? Do they think it's Brad or is this just a formality? And if this is Brad and he has been found, does it mean this is finally over?* I hated myself for thinking it but the thought kept echoing. *Am I so desperate for a resolution that I will accept this fate for Brad so easily?*

I found Anna's car in its usual spot in the parking lot and fumbled with her keys as I unlocked the passenger side door. I plopped into the familiar seat and noticed a printed photo next to the speedometer that hadn't been there before. The picture of Anna, Thomas, Brad and I had been taken before one of the school soccer games in the spring. We were huddled together, smiling and making various hand gestures towards the camera.

As hard as I tried, I couldn't remember who had taken the photo. I just remembered how great that night, and all the others we spent together, had been and how much I had taken them for granted. The sudden appearance of this photo on the dash made me wonder if Anna was hurting more than I had given her credit for. *What are those words from Chris' book? We all show pain in different ways.*

I jumped as Anna jerked open the driver's side door, slamming it behind her as she sat.

"Okay, I think I got all of your stuff."

I traded for her keys as she handed me my textbook and a handful of pencils and highlighters.

"Where can we go?" I asked as she started the engine.

"Your house?"

I grimaced thinking back to my mother's threats of lifelong grounding if I skipped anymore school. *Surely she will make an exception for this situation.*

"Okay."

Anna pulled out of the parking lot and stepped on the gas as soon as she was out of sight of school grounds. It had only been a few weeks since we had spent time together, but the awkward silence in the car made it seem like much longer. I looked back to the photo of all of us together. We looked younger. We looked happier. I decided I was done taking the time I had with the ones I loved for granted. I was anxious to ask more about what information she had gotten from her mom, but something else had to happen first.

"Anna," I said. "Listen, I'm really sorry about everything before."

"Don't even worry about it, Lil. It's not important."

"I'm having a really hard time with all of this." I glanced at her out of the corner of my eye. She was nodding.

"Yeah, I know. I am too. I was just…trying to hide it." Her voice broke. "I guess I thought if I ignored it, it wouldn't seem real."

Ignoring it had never been an option for me. The part of me Brad took with him when he disappeared was much too big.

"But this," Anna continued. "This is *so* real. I'm so scared."

"What did your mom tell you?" I asked. "I mean, do they really think the person they found is Brad?"

"I don't know. She didn't seem to have much information and I don't think the police have said much to Mrs. Lee yet, either. She just said she wanted us to know before we found out from the afternoon news."

Anna turned onto our street as she spoke. We weren't halfway down the driveway before my mom came running out of the house. The gruesome discovery of the body of an adult male wouldn't be waiting until the five o' clock broadcast. Brad's story was breaking news.

# 11

## dental records

BRAD'S CASE HAD ONLY GOTTEN ONE MENTION
on our local news station at the time of his disappearance, yet
suddenly with the discovery of a body just a few miles outside
of Lions Port, every station in the state was hot on the story.

*Human remains found by hunters in Morris County may be those of
missing high school graduate Bradley Lee, who vanished the night of his
graduation ceremony on May sixteenth. The remains were discovered in an
advanced state of decomposition but they have been determined to be that of
an adult male, between five foot ten and six feet. The cause of death is
being investigated and the Morris County coroner will determine if these
remains are, in fact, those of the missing teen.*

Every station showed the cropped photo of us at prom

from his Have You Seen This Man poster, and occasionally they used the full picture with my face blurred out. Seeing the pixilation over my head was hard, but hearing the commentary provided by the newscasters was much worse.

*"I'm learning that the missing teen, Brad Lee, has an extensive juvenile record and law enforcement suspect he may have been involved with drug related trade at the time of his disappearance."*

*"The body was found in an isolated wooded area, over one and a half miles from any main roads. There is speculation as to whether the deceased was transported to that location."*

*"Investigators are saying they cannot confirm or deny, based on evidence at the scene, if foul play is involved."*

*"The question on everyone's mind tonight—how does a teenager's body end up decomposed in a lean-to tent in the middle of the woods?"*

The facts were presented to us through the media almost as frequently as through Detective Padron, and we would often hear mixed messages and look to law enforcement to confirm the actual details. *Was the body found under a tarp, or wrapped in a tarp? Was there evidence the body had been there for some time or is it a presumed body dump?* We were asking questions I had never imagined asking in my wildest dreams. It was funny that once a person's remains were referred to as 'a body' they didn't seem like an actual human being who was once living and breathing. 'A body' didn't leave behind loved ones desperate for answers and confirmation of identity. But a person did. Brad did.

After two days of being planted in front of the television with my laptop by my side and phone in hand, they still had not confirmed if the remains that had been found were those of Brad. I hadn't cried. I remained in a constant state of feeling like I was holding my breath under water. No one was saying it, but I felt certain that everyone was having the same guilty thoughts that I had the first moment I heard about the discovery. No one wanted this to be him, but everyone wanted answers.

What we knew was that a body, determined to be that of a male between the ages of sixteen and twenty-five, was found in the woods underneath a tarp that had been strung between a cluster of trees to create a shelter. Around the shelter and the campsite were various items that were considered evidence and being fingerprinted, and a small fire pit full of ashes indicating that the person had been staying there for some time.

The deceased had been dead for a minimum of a few weeks, but the state of decomposition was hard to determine because of the extreme summer heat that had been magnified by the plastic tarp. Based on the condition of the body, there were no fingerprints to be collected, no birthmarks to be found, and no eye color to match. The facial structure was beyond recognition and the Lees had not been asked to identify the body. Instead, what they were asked for was a copy of Brad's dental records and a sample of his DNA, which came in the form of his toothbrush that had spent the last four months lying next to the sink in the Lees second-floor bathroom.

"It will take time," Detective Padron told us.

What they weren't saying on the news was that the body had been found less than a mile from Lizard's shop. The day I went to Lizard's I had walked right past the path that led the hunters to the campsite. Detective Padron had questioned him, but other than the proximity of the location there was nothing found that tied him to the body or the tent. *Lizard may have failed out of high school, but he isn't dumb enough to leave behind evidence that might link him to a possible crime. But then he also isn't dumb enough to dump a body right up the road from where he works. But maybe he is that arrogant?*

I couldn't decide if I thought Lizard was a killer. *And if Lizard is bitter enough to kill anyone…why wouldn't it have been me?* The police released him but told him not to leave town. It was a formality, but I found it laughable. *Lizard has never left this town and never will.*

****

Pastor Allen planned a vigil at church on Friday night so people could come to light candles and pray. Hundreds of people from around town attended and stood in the church lawn holding glowing white candles inside of tiny plastic cups to catch the dripping wax. The moon was only a sliver that night and the flickering flames lit up the sky. It was truly beautiful, like something out of a movie, in a heartbreaking kind of way.

I positioned myself behind everyone else, separated from my family and friends, wanting to be able to see everything and everyone. I was on the look out for Lizard, although I wasn't surprised when I couldn't find him in the crowd. I figured he could just as easily be lurking in the shadows of the trees surrounding the churchyard if he wanted to take a peek at the action. I also kept my eyes peeled for Chris. I knew it was a long shot, but I desperately wanted to find his smiling face in the sea of people. He would know just the right thing to say.

"We thank all of you for continuing to support us and pray for Brad's safe return." Mr. Lee addressed everyone with Janice and Montana by his side. "While we pray that this young man that has been discovered is not our son, he is *someone's* son. We have to trust God's plan and trust that the truth will be revealed to us in His time. Although Brad had some stumbles along his path, God does not love him any less."

He opened up the microphone to Janice and she continued to thank everyone for their support and attendance. I hung on the words 'some stumbles along his path'. *Everyone stumbles. Why does he have to have excuses made for him?* News crews were set up around the perimeter of the church, filming the Lees as they delivered their speeches. Big haired reporters primped and rehearsed their lead-ins, preparing for live feed and undoubtedly hoping for a chance to interview the family. It made me angry that the discovery of the body had suddenly made this a newsworthy story when the initial disappearance of a young man that was loved by his friends and family hadn't drawn any interest. *Reporters are attracted to death just like flies.*

Anna found me in the crowd and wrapped her arms around me.

"I wish you would have agreed to sing," she said.

"No," I whispered, shaking my head. "I couldn't."

"I get it. How are you doing?"

I shrugged. "They never want to interview me," I told her as I motioned towards the string of reporters.

"I'm sure they would if you asked. Do you want them to interview you?"

I shrugged again. *What could I say that would matter?* "I don't know," I said softly, reaching for Brad's ring. "I guess I just expected they would ask."

"I understand. I'm sorry."

I grimaced. Anna didn't know any better, but I had been swearing to myself that I would scream if one more person told me they were sorry. *What is everyone so sorry for? Sorry for not taking this case more seriously before it became the lead-in on every newscast? Or are they truly sorry because they realize this is the hardest thing I have ever gone through? Are they sorry because they can't possibly understand the pain of living in constant limbo and those two little words are the only thing they can come up with to say to me?*

"It looks like they are just finishing up." Anna broke my train of thought. "I'm going to go say hi to Mr. and Mrs. Lee."

"Okay."

I followed behind her as she made her way through the dispersing crowd still holding their glowing candles. The Lees had decided not to release balloons or butterflies or have people leave flowers and teddy bears around a framed photo of Brad. Instead, everyone was asked to use their candle to light another in their own home and keep the flame burning for Brad. It was a romantic idea, and would be a beautiful gesture in many homes around town, but also sounded like a fire hazard.

Reporters flocked toward the Lees as Anna and I approached them. I waved to Montana once I caught her eye; her face lit up when she saw me. She tugged on her dad's sleeve as she pointed at me.

"Okay, you can go talk to Lillian. Just stay close," he said, kissing her on the forehead.

As I watched her walk towards me, I thought of how terrifying it must be for her family to let her out of their sight. If all six feet, one hundred ninety pounds of their son could vanish into thin air, anything could happen to their petite, naïve daughter.

"Hi, Lillian." Montana threw her arms around my waist and pressed her face into my gut. I squeezed her tiny frame as I ran my hand over her strawberry blonde curls.

"Hi, sweetie. How are you doing?"

"I'm okay." She pulled away from our hug and gave me a half smile, turning up the corner of one side of her mouth.

"Yeah." I nodded. "I'm okay too."

"The candles are pretty." She looked out across the lawn where some of my classmates and acquaintances still remained. Mandy, along with Tess and Thomas, stood several yards away in a semi-circle, holding what remained of their candles. Mandy appeared to be crying as her boyfriend, Parker, rubbed her shoulders.

"They are very pretty." I looked back to Montana. "Brad would probably say they are a little too girly, though, huh?"

A large, toothless grin grew on her face for a moment before her eyes welled up with tears. "I really miss him," she said, wiping her cheek with the back of her hand.

I pulled her in close to me again. "I really miss him too."

"He still feels like a real brother to me," she mumbled.

My ears perked up. "Montana, what did you say?" I wasn't sure if I had heard her correctly. I held her shoulders; the light of the candles around us flickered in her innocent eyes.

"What do you mean, real brother?" I asked, searching her face. The words were no louder than a whisper as they left my lips.

"What?" she asked, dumbfounded. *Did I imagine it?*

"I thought you said…"

"Montana!" I was interrupted by Janice's call. "Come say goodbye to Pastor Allen."

"Gotta go," she said. "Bye, Lillian."

Before I had a chance to stop her she slipped into the crowd and was out of reach.

"I need to be getting home, too. Do you want a ride?" Anna asked as she approached.

"Um…" I watched as Mrs. Lee was summoned by a red-headed reporter who was waving a block-shaped microphone in her direction. "Yeah. Let me just tell my parents."

I knew it wasn't the right time to be asking questions. After we found my dad in the crowd, Anna and I walked slowly to her car, carrying our candles and attempting to protect the flames from the cool night breeze by sheltering them with our hands. I stared into the glowing light and my mind drifted away. *Just how many secrets was Brad keeping from me?*

"Lillian?"

I jerked my head up to look at Anna. Her eyes were moist.

"Yeah?"

"Do you think it's him?"

We hadn't asked each other this daunting question before. *Do I think it could be him? Maybe. Do I want it to be him? I don't think so. Do I hope it isn't him? Of course. If this isn't him, how much longer do I think I can go on not knowing? I have no idea.*

I sighed. "I don't know, Anna. None of this makes any sense."

She nodded and wiped a small droplet from her eye. "Thomas thinks that it is. I mean, he hasn't said it but I know that's what he is thinking. That's why he didn't want to come with me tonight. I had to beg him to even show up."

We reached the car and I pulled the unlocked passenger door open.

"What do you think?" I asked. *Why don't they prepare us for situations like this in school? Why do we have to learn about Aztecs and Mayans from centuries ago when we aren't taught how to deal with real life?*

"I think you're right," she said with a nod. "It doesn't make any sense. Why would Brad have been living under a tarp in the woods by Lizard's shop? What would he have possibly needed to escape from that would have made him do something like that?" She started the car and pulled onto the street in front of our church, handing me her glowing candle.

"Did you ever hear anything about Brad being adopted?" I asked her.

"Adopted?" Anna took her eyes off the road for a moment and looked at me with her eyebrows raised. "Brad? No. Why?"

"I don't know…" I shook my head. "Just something Montana said tonight that sounded weird. It's probably nothing."

"If Brad were adopted wouldn't he have told you that?"

"I'd think so…yeah." *Not necessarily. He certainly didn't tell me about the time he spent in juvenile court.*

Anna didn't respond, and I didn't elaborate on what

Montana had said. I wasn't sure if we had run out of things to say or if we were both lost in our thoughts about Brad, but we spent the rest of the drive in silence.

****

Anna dropped me off in my driveway and we said our goodbyes. The house was dark, illuminated only by the streetlight. I figured my parents must still be at the vigil shaking hands with fellow congregation members, or picking up Graham and Eliza from the sitter. My candle flickered as I made my way down the dark sidewalk to the front steps. The only thing I could hear was the scrape of my feet against the pavement. The night air seemed quieter than usual; as though the entire town was inside their homes lighting candles for Brad.

I squinted as I approached the door, the flickering flame in my hand cast tall, eerie shadows against the bricks. A chill ran up my spine. Something didn't seem right. Suddenly, a dark figure rose up in front of me.

"Hey," a deep voice said as I let out a squeal.

I could just make out the silhouette of a tall man in the darkness. He was familiar.

"Chris?" I whispered as I extended my candle towards him.

"What? No. It's me." There was the click of a flashlight and a garish light illuminated his face from beneath his chin. "Lizard."

My heart dropped. I looked down the street out of the corner of my eye but there was no sign of headlights. We were alone in the dark. *I am alone in the dark with a potential killer. And he knows I'm the one who sold him out to the police.*

"Lizard?" I pushed in front of him and felt my way up the steps as I fumbled for my key in my pocket. "What are you doing here?"

I forced the key into the lock and swung the door open just far enough so I could reach my arm inside and find the light switch with my fingertips. A burst of bright yellow light lit up the house.

"I saw the news. About the…about the body."

"Come on, Lizard. You didn't *see the news*," I snapped. "You found out when Detective Padron came pounding on your door."

"They know I had nothin' to do with it." He was defensive yet vulnerable. He didn't seem so tough in the golden glow of the porch light.

"You missed the vigil tonight," I told him, taking one step closer.

"The people at that church don't want me comin' 'round after this stuff came out about me."

"You don't know that," I said with a shrug.

"Lillian," he continued. There was a weakness in his voice. "I know I messed up when I didn't tell the police about that guy who came lookin' for Brad."

I was tempted to agree with him, but I held my tongue and listened. There was a look in his eyes I recognized. *Pain.*

"I wasn't takin' this whole thing seriously. I thought all you folks were just makin' a huge deal out of nothin' and he would be showin' back up." He stopped to clear his throat. "But if this guy they found in the woods *right by my place* is Brad and he was there this whole time…"

The torment on his face and in his voice was almost unbearable. I imagined this must be how people had seen me the past four months. *This is why people avoid me. They can't see past my pain.*

He reached into his breast pocket and pulled out a single cigarette and a lighter. The flame flickered as he drew a deep breath.

"You were right," he said with a cough, smoke pouring from his nostrils. "I know why he chose you over me."

I looked down at my tennis shoes. There were scuffs of dirt on the toes from traipsing through muddy fields looking for Brad. *We were looking in all the wrong places.*

"Lillian, you know I didn't have anythin' to do with this," he insisted. "Right?

I peered up at him and once again saw the same glimmer-less look in his eyes I recognized from my reflection in the mirror. I nodded. "I know."

"Brad's a good guy. He doesn't deserve this." Lizard puffed on the cigarette again and a cloud of smoke hit my face.

"None of us deserve this," I whispered.

He took a final drag and tipped his head to me.

"Anyway, I just wanted to tell you I'm sorry. I hope it ain't him."

"Thanks, Lizard."

I watched him for a moment as he headed into the front yard taking long, quick strides towards the street. It was the same path Brad would have taken that final night. I had once wished it had been Lizard that disappeared instead of Brad. But watching him move, with his shoulders hanging low and smoke billowing from the cigarette between his fingers, I knew he didn't deserve that fate. Just like Brad, Lizard was someone's son, grandson, or maybe even brother. And no matter what his past said about him he deserved to live a life like the rest of us. Uninterrupted. *Unbroken.*

# 12

## the life and death of brad lee

THERE WAS AN ENTIRE WEEK OF SILENCE. NO updates on the body, no tips, no leads, just a haunting stillness that sometimes tricked me into believing it was all a dream when I woke up in the morning. A quick glance across to the room to the stack of Have You Seen This Man posters on my dresser was always sure to remind me it was real. Brad was still gone.

I went through all the motions of a typical weekly routine, attending every class and attempting to socialize with Anna and our group of friends in the afternoons, although I jumped every time a phone rang in my vicinity. The discovery of the body had changed the dynamic between me and my friends.

They showed more compassion towards me and I did my best not to take advantage of their friendship. They were starting to understand what I had been going through since the first morning I learned Brad was missing. Realizing there was a possibility that a member of our little group was dead made the whole situation seem more real to them. Just like the news reporters, my friends were awakened by death.

When I wasn't with Anna and the others I was sitting on my bed glued to my laptop, typing gruesome topics into the search engine like *identifying a corpse* and *are dental records always accurate*. But while skimming through countless blogs about levels of decomposition and the autopsy process, and attempting to avoid any photos on the topics, my mind kept wandering to a different subject. *Adoption.*

I searched for *accessing adoption records* and waded through dozens of websites; only to discover that answers to the lists of frequently asked questions were always the same. *The person whose information will be disclosed must consent to the disclosure.* The Internet had always seemed like an endless source of knowledge before Brad went missing. But now it felt like every click of the mouse opened up another virtual brick wall.

****

I spent the first half of the day on Saturday morning staring at the living room TV screen from the corner of the couch, watching colorful animals dance around odd-shaped children as Graham and Eliza sat immersed in their usual morning cartoons. I could hear the characters speaking and singing but the words sounded like white noise. My forehead was pounding, only I didn't have the energy to go to the kitchen in search of a pain reliever. I just kept staring at the television, concentrating so hard on the screen that I hoped I might be teleported into the magical rainbow world. *Just until I have answers.*

The ringer suddenly cried out from the landline phone that sat on the end table beside me, and I was snapped back into reality. I yanked the receiver off the hook and blurted a jumbled 'Hello!' into the telephone.

"Lillian?" The raspy voice was familiar.

"Yes, this is she." I pulled the phone away from my face and slapped my hand over the mouthpiece. "Guys, turn that down!" I hissed at Graham and Eliza.

"Lillian, it's Detective Padron. Janice Lee requested I call you." He sounded calm. Too calm.

"Yes? Has the...the body been identified?" My heart was racing so quickly that it caused Brad's ring to vibrate against my chest.

"Yes, we were able to confirm the identity based on the dental records."

"Is it him?" I wanted to shout but the words came out as a squeak. *Please, Lord.*

"Lillian," he paused and I held my breath. Graham and Eliza were staring at me, frozen on top of their pillows on the floor, their faces scrunched with anticipation. Detective Padron cleared his throat and I clutched tighter onto the phone. *Answer me!*

"It's not him," he finally said.

I felt all of the air leave my body—as if a semi-truck had slammed into my gut. "It's not him?" I repeated.

"It's not Brad. The body is that of another young man who ran away from home early this year. It doesn't seem to be connected to Brad's disappearance in any way…"

He continued to speak as my eyes flooded with tears that began streaming uncontrollably down my cheeks. I managed to thank him and say goodbye through my sobbing, but after hanging up the phone my face dropped into my hands. I cried harder when I realized that I didn't know why I was crying. I wasn't sad. I wasn't happy. My most prominent emotion was anger.

"Aren't you glad?" Eliza asked in an innocent voice as she came and sat beside me on the couch. *No eight-year-old should have to comfort her sister because the body that was found isn't her boyfriend's.*

"Yes." I looked up at her with blurry eyes. "It's good, right?"

*But it doesn't feel good.* My nose began to run as tears continued to drip down my face. I had nothing. He was still missing. The week I had spent attempting to accept the idea of Brad being gone forever had been in vain. And I hated myself for wishing it had been him in that tent.

****

There seemed to be a cloud over the Sunday morning church service. We opened with prayers for Brad but Pastor Allen quickly diverted to his pre-planned sermon about God's timing and trusting His plans. I knew it could easily be related to Brad, but I tried to tune it out. I didn't want to listen to talk of timing and plans that meant Brad would remain missing. I was struggling with the fact that I was supposed to trust God's plan if it meant I would have to keep on living with a hole in my heart.

I thought back to a sermon from months earlier when Pastor Allen preached about believing in prayers and that they would be answered. *I have been saying the same prayer every day for nearly four and half months and it hasn't been answered, so what am I doing wrong? Do I truly believe he will be found when I pray? Do I truly believe anything anymore?*

After a final song, the congregation was dismissed and Mrs. Lee lingered on the front row pew as Montana followed her dad out of the sanctuary. *This is my chance.*

"Janice?" I put my hand on her back as I approached her.

"Lillian!" She turned her head towards me and smiled. "How are you today, sweetheart?"

"I'm okay," I said with a shrug. "But I was...I was hoping I could talk to you for a few minutes?" I picked awkwardly at the trim of my blouse.

"Of course. Let me grab my things and I'll meet you outside."

"Thanks." I nodded.

I sent my family ahead without me before making my way into the prayer garden in the church courtyard and sitting on a gliding wooden bench. I pushed my feet against the mulch to propel the seat back and forth. Brad and I had often sat on this same bench after Sunday school or youth group. Once in the spring, we left the school basketball game just before half time, ventured down the street to the church and snuggled up on the bench beneath an old flannel blanket. We could hear the marching band playing even from the garden, the instruments carried out of the gym and through the peaceful night air. It was one of the first nights I suspected he might be falling in love with me, and I with him. *What kind of guy leaves a tied game to find a quiet place to sit with his sports-illiterate girlfriend?* Brad was that kind of guy. *Is that kind of guy...*

"There you are!" Mrs. Lee exclaimed with a laugh as she came around the corner of the church.

"Sorry," I replied, standing. "This was our spot."

"I remember." She motioned towards the bench and I lowered myself back onto the seat. As she sat down next to me she placed her hand on my knee. "I always knew where to find you two after the service." A wave of sadness washed over her face.

"Thank you..." I swallowed. "Thank you for having Detective Padron call me."

"Of course. It was big news."

"Have you heard anything else? Or gotten any new leads through the website or social media pages?"

She shook her head. "Sightings come in here and there but nothing has panned out. It's nice to know people are on the lookout, just hard not to get our hopes up every time someone thinks they saw Brad in a laundry mat or riding the bus somewhere. But I promise you'll be the first person we call as soon as anything seems promising."

"Thanks."

"How are you holding up?" she asked with a motherly tone in her voice. "Is there anything I can do?"

"Well, actually..." I searched her eyes as I tried to find the words to say. "There's something I have been wanting to ask you."

"Sure, hun." The corners of her mouth formed a small smile as she waited for me to speak.

Seeing her smile, I suddenly felt as though my tongue had been glued to the roof of my mouth and my words were trapped behind my lips. *Is this my life now? Interrogating my boyfriend's mother about details he should have told me himself? If it's true, what will she say when she finds out I didn't know?*

"Lillian?" Janice's face was kind as she quietly said my name. I realized that in the last several months I hadn't looked at her very closely. Despite Brad's absence, she maintained a glow. I could see she was much stronger than I was.

"You know you can ask me anything," she said, nudging my shoulder. My question was bouncing around on my tongue.

"Was Brad adopted?" I finally blurted out.

I watched as her eyes grew wide. She held her breath for a moment before she spoke.

"He didn't tell you?"

As I shook my head my heart sank. It was true. Brad was gone, and I felt like the laughingstock of the town—the girl whose life was on hold waiting for the guy she seemingly knew nothing about.

"I'm sorry you didn't know, Lillian. It was always a very sensitive subject for him."

"So, what...I mean, what happened that made you adopt him?" I wasn't sure what the important questions were. *What does this mean?*

"We were living in Missouri at the time, and had never dreamed of adopting an older child, but he came to our church through an outreach ministry that was witnessing to children in group homes and he just broke our hearts. His left arm was broken and his head had been shaved because he'd contracted lice…he was so thin and pale. We were told his mother was an addict and she had given him up willingly. She chose her habit over her child."

I couldn't find any words to say. I had always pictured Brad's childhood as a privileged one, but now my mind was forming an image of an emaciated boy in a wrapped cast being abandoned. I suddenly understood why he hadn't told me. *He didn't want me to see him as unwanted.*

"I always worried that church reminded him of those days in the group home. Like being here made him feel like he was that sick, orphaned boy again." She shook her head. "That's why I never forced him to join us. It wanted it to be his decision to come. I was grateful to you for finally getting him involved."

"He liked coming here," I assured her.

"He liked going anywhere with you," she said with a broken smile.

*And I would have followed him to the edge of the earth.*

"We moved here soon after the adoption was finalized," she continued. "Brad needed a new start, and we chose not to disclose his adoption unless necessary. He didn't want to broadcast it and we agreed it wasn't right to share it with everyone in our new town. We thought it might change the way people saw him and treated him if they knew the truth."

"But do the police know…" My mind and my mouth were working independently. Neither could catch up with the other.

"Yes, we told Detective Padron, and some of the other officers have known his situation ever since he started getting in trouble with the law. But we have asked them not to make it public unless it has something to do with a hard lead in the case. Brad has had enough of his dirty laundry exposed since he went missing. We don't want this to come out, too."

I nodded. The town didn't need another reason to turn Brad's life story into a reality TV show.

"Did Brad ever try to find his Mom?" I asked. "Is there a chance that's where he is…?"

She shook her head. "We searched his laptop, went through his emails and browsing history…there was nothing to give us the impression that he was looking for her. And he was spending all of his free time with you, so it's hard to imagine that he would have been able to search for her without any of us knowing."

That thought almost made me smile, but it was shrouded in too much mystery. *How did he manage to spend all of his spare time with me while keeping so many secrets?*

"We've looked for her, his biological mother, and so have the police, but the last record of her is from a Missouri jail three years ago. She is practically a missing person, too."

*Like mother, like son.*

"And the man that came to Lizard's asking for Brad before he disappeared, could that be his real dad?"

"No one knows who Brad's biological father is, not even his mother as far as I know. We aren't sure how, or if, that man Lizard talked to is connected to any of this."

Just as soon as the door to new possibilities had been

opened it was collapsing in on itself. *Can the truth about Brad's childhood and family really just be another secret he had kept hidden from me?*

"We still have no idea exactly what Brad went through before he came to live with us. But he was holding onto a lot of anger towards his biological mother for abandoning him the way she did. That anger needed outlets, and those outlets came in the form of theft and vandalism and befriending others that shared the same tortured souls. And then he found you."

"What do you mean?" I asked, fiddling with Brad's ring under the neck of my shirt.

"All these things Brad didn't tell you about his past…don't see them as a reflection of how he felt about you," she told me. "When you came into his life you helped him escape a very troubled path. He wanted to be clean and new and I think his relationship with you made him feel that way. I just don't think he wanted to burden you with the truth about his past. What if it changed how you felt about him, how you saw him?"

"But it doesn't."

"I know that. And you know that. But maybe it wasn't a risk he was willing to take." Janice shifted her body towards mine on the bench and leaned in closer so our eyes were level. "Brad didn't talk to me much about his feelings for you, and I didn't ask – partially because I wanted to respect his privacy and partially because I didn't need to. The love he felt for you was written all over his face twenty-four hours a day. It changed the way he talked, the way he moved…it energized him. I will be forever grateful to you for the impact you had on

Brad's life." She blinked back tears as she let out a deep sigh.

"But sometimes," she continued. "I worry that there was only so much that any of us could do to repair the damage inside. And knowing that his biological mother wasn't there to watch him graduate might have triggered that pent up anger..."

Her head dropped for just a moment, as though she was giving in to a fleeting ounce of weakness. But just as soon as she had let down her guard her shoulders pulled back and she held her chin high.

"You changed his life, and you have the ability to do that for so many other people. You continue to see the good even when all you hear is bad. No matter what the outcome of this is...please don't let it break your spirit."

I tried to nod but my head was heavy. It seemed apparent to her, just as it had been to Chris, that I had broken down.

"I truly believe that Brad made choices that got him to wherever he is today," she went on. "They might have been very tough choices to make, or choices he knew were wrong, but he made choices. You can make choices too. Brad would want you to make the right choices."

*If he did make choices, only one can be certain. He didn't choose me.*

She stood up and pulled her purse over her shoulder as she turned to face me.

"I should get going, I'm sure Montana is getting anxious. Can we give you a ride home?"

"No, thank you. I'm going to stay for a little while."

"Okay, be careful getting home. And think about what I said, okay, Lillian?" she said with a smile. "*Choices.*"

"I will."

I leaned into the corner of the bench and watched as she stepped carefully through the grass and disappeared behind the church. *Choices.* The word kept echoing in my mind. *Choices.* Brad chose to abandon his past and the memory of the mother who had abandoned him. And he hadn't just kept it a secret from me, it was a secret engineered to be kept from our entire town. *If the Lees moved Brad to Lions Port to start a new life, did he simply decide he wanted to start over again after graduation and walk away? Was that the choice?*

Brad always had a certain amount of mystery behind his eyes, but I was realizing he was much more complicated than I could ever have imagined. He had done a wonderful job putting on the façade of a perfect boyfriend, son, and student. *But how much of it was a lie? How much of it was the truth?*

# 13

## normalization process: in progress

ONCE THE WORD GOT OUT THAT THE BODY wasn't Brad, his story quickly became old news. Instead, the television was racked with reports of James Morgan, the runaway from Fayetteville who had overdosed in his makeshift campsite. Occasionally, news anchors threw around Brad's name as they debated whether he had met the same fate as young James, but there was a lack of compassion in their voices. There was no more excitement, no new gruesome discoveries of decaying flesh, no updates that warranted a report. Brad was once again becoming that 'first-name last name missing guy' that people easily forgot about.

After church on Sunday, I searched the town for any sign

of Chris, but he was nowhere to be found. I spoke to the frizzy haired waitress at the diner, asking if she remembered seeing him in the past few weeks. But she shook her head and pointed towards the bulletin board where Brad's poster hung.

"You're welcome to put up a flyer if you can't find your friend," she said in a cheerful voice.

"That won't be necessary," I told her.

Later that afternoon I plugged his first and last name into various people-finding search engines, again to no avail. I found a man named Chris Colvin who worked as a chiropractor in Lincoln, Nebraska, and a sixty-eight-year-old Christopher Colvin who had been arrested in New Jersey for drunk driving, but no teenage, blue-eyed boy.

My parents let me miss school on Monday as I continued to come to terms with the fact that Brad was still missing. Anna called that morning to announce she would pick up my assignments and bring them by after class dismissed, with a reminder that she was there for me and all of our friends were thinking of me. She kept repeating how glad she was that the body wasn't Brad, but I couldn't share her enthusiasm.

I lay in bed for most of the morning, my mind racing with the thoughts of everything I had lost. I had lost Brad, but along with that came the loss of time, energy, strength and ambition. And then there was my faith. *Why would God allow something like this to happen? Have I lost my faith? Or is it all I have left?*

I skimmed through the book Chris gave me that I kept in the drawer of my bedside table. I hadn't been able to make it through more than a few pages, and every time I opened it I wondered why he had given it to me. Everything the book talked about was death, which was much more final than my situation. Had it been Brad's body in that tent the book would have been helpful, but there was no chapter for coping with the pain of a missing loved one. There were no paragraphs about holding on to hope while maintaining a normal life.

I started to fold the book shut when a word caught my eye. *Pain.* I looked closer and read the sentence out loud.

"*When the pain doesn't go away, we must find ways to push it to the back.*"

I read it to myself again. *How do you push it to the back? What is the secret?*

I continued reading, taking in every other word until I found the sentence that spoke to me.

*Even if it is difficult, you must try to normalize your life as much as you can. Even if you can't do something as well as you once could, you have to keep trying.*

I folded the corner of the page and dropped the book into my lap. The initial thought of 'normalizing' my life seemed so daunting. I thought back to the nights I had spent with my friends while we were waiting for the body to be identified. They made me feel comforted and safe—like we were in this together. With them, it actually seemed possible that I could go on living, being a student, and a friend, and have a somewhat normal life even if Brad was gone. I probably wouldn't be as good of a student as I had once been, but as the book said, I had to keep trying. Janice's words from the day before came into my mind. *You can make choices too, Lillian. But can I really push the pain to the back and live a normal life again?*

I crawled deeper into my bed, pulled the covers up to my chin, and closed my eyes. I searched for the words I wanted to pray. It was hard to convince myself that it would even do any good when my prayers hadn't been answered up until now. Continuing to pray a prayer that remained so unresolved had left me angry, feeling betrayed and confused. But it was time to change my request. *Please help me find what I am looking for, whether it is Brad or something else. Please don't let me keep hurting all the time. Show me how to live a life that feels somewhat normal, whatever that means.*

****

I didn't sleep through the night, a reoccurring dream of Brad showing up at our high school and joining the football team kept making its way into my mind. But I got up early and took a long, hot shower as I prepared for the school day. Wrapped in two towels, one across my hair and the other around my body, I pushed the pile of clothes that had gathered on my vanity stool to the floor and sat in front of the lighted mirror.

I remembered sitting in the same exact spot for hours while preparing for dates with Brad. Trash and clutter had accumulated on top of the vanity table as it had sat unused since May. But beneath the discards were the dozens of tiny but beautiful bottles of perfume I always requested at Christmas time, bins of drugstore makeup I had once loved to experiment with along with Anna, and countless tubes of hair products and lotion. Looking at the scattered array of beauty products made me smile. *I can do this.*

I blow-dried my hair and ran a straightener over the ends before pinning a few long strands away from my face. I hadn't taken the time to notice how much my hair had grown over the summer and was surprised to find it fell halfway down my back when it wasn't hastily thrown into a ponytail. After rummaging through unorganized makeup, I found everything I needed for a quick, natural face like I had typically worn to school the year before. I applied a dab of extra concealer under each eye to hide the bags that had developed since May.

Hanging in the back of my closet were several brightly colored tops that my mom had purchased for me in a summer sale at the department store where she worked. I decided on a purple and green chevron blouse and paired it with denim capris and the jeweled, tan sandals I had worn the previous summer for weeks on end.

Standing in front of my full-length mirror, I almost gasped when I saw my reflection. Looking back at me was a beautiful young woman I hardly recognized. My skin looked a bit paler, and my eyes seemed heavier, but there I was. If I hadn't known any better I may have thought I was myself on the day of Brad's graduation, carefree and hungry for life. I hoped it wasn't too late to feel that way again.

I lifted my book bag from the floor and walked slowly down the hallway. Mom's back was to me as I entered the kitchen; she stood over the stove watching scrambled eggs as they fried in the pan. My bag made a gentle *thud* as I dropped it onto the tile. When she heard the noise she turned towards me and a smile grew on her face.

"Look at you! You look beautiful. I knew that top would fit you perfectly," she told me with a nod. "Breakfast is almost ready. Your dad took the kids to get doughnuts before school because of some silly bet the three of them had going."

"Thanks, Mom." I poured myself a cup of coffee with a splash of vanilla creamer and leaned up against the counter. Mom shoveled fluffy, yellow eggs onto two small plates and topped them off with strips of bacon.

"Is Anna picking you up or do you need a ride?" she asked as she carried the plates to the table, passing me a fork once we sat down across from each other.

"She'll be here soon," I said, picking up a piece of bacon with my fingertips. "Thanks for making this."

Mom nodded as she chewed a forkful of eggs and we spent the next few minutes in silence, aside from the sound of our metal forks hitting the ceramic plates.

"I know you don't want to talk about college," she said suddenly. "But I still don't think it's something you can just write off and…"

"Mom. We can talk about it soon, okay." I put down my fork. "Just not yet."

"Lillian, the longer you wait your options are going to become fewer and fewer…"

"I'm not ready." I was tempted to raise my voice, but I held myself back. "I'm really, *really* trying here. Please just give me some more time."

I pushed my chair back from the table and collected my bag from the floor. When I looked up I could tell she was eyeing Brad's ring hanging around my neck.

"Okay," she agreed with a nod. "I'll give you more time."

"Thanks. I'll see you tonight."

"I love you, Lillian," she said from her chair.

"I love you too, Mom," I replied as I placed my plate and fork in the dishwasher.

Thoughts ran through my head as I went out the side door and waited for Anna under the carport. *I truly do love her and I know she only wants what's best for me. I should tell her that more often. I should tell everyone in my family, and my friends, how much I care about them. Life is too short not to.*

Anna's blue car sped into the driveway and she peered over her sunglasses as I opened the passenger side door.

"Who are you and what are you doing in my car?" she asked with a laugh.

"Very funny." I smiled back, gesturing at my new top. "You like?"

"Okay, seriously, you look awesome. You know you do! And yes, I want to borrow that shirt like, now!"

"Thanks. Just something new I'm trying out."

"Well let me tell you something, girl." Anna put the car in reverse and hit the gas as she stared into the rearview. "It's working for you."

I laughed and we turned up the radio when a familiar song came on, both of us singing along at the top of our lungs as we drove. I looked to her when it ended and fiddled with the volume knob.

"I was wondering about something."

"Yeah, what?" she asked, keeping her eyes on the road.

"Does Caleb Marino have a date for the fall social yet?"

Anna pulled up to a red stoplight and jerked her head towards me with her eyebrows raised.

"That's funny. It sounded like you just asked if Caleb has a date for the fall social…but I must have misheard you."

"Come on. Does he?" I rolled my eyes.

"He, in fact, does *not* to the best of my knowledge. Can I ask why you want to know? Asking for a friend, I assume?" She grinned as she accelerated again and headed toward the school parking lot.

"I'd like to go with you guys. If it's not too late. I'm sorry I said no before. I just…"

"You don't have to explain." We pulled into her parking space and she smiled at me as she turned off the engine. "It's going to be so much fun. I'm so glad you want to go!"

"Me too." I collected my bag from the floorboard but stopped myself before I reached for the door handle. "Anna, thanks for being my friend through all of this."

She looked at me with her lips pursed. "No, thank you for being *my* friend through all of this. I'm sorry I couldn't always understand what you were going through."

"Consider yourself lucky," I said with a stone face that slowly grew into a smile. "Come on."

We walked arm in arm to the school doors and I took a deep breath as Anna tugged on the handle. *Here's to normal.*

****

I stayed alert through my classes, attempted to joke and laugh with my friends at lunch, and even auditioned for a solo in choir. After school let out I went shopping with Anna and Mandy for dresses to wear to the social. I didn't try anything on, I wasn't quite there yet, but I watched as they twirled around in dozens of formal dresses in the department store, oohing and aahing over the sequins and jewels.

"Can I plan something for all of us for this weekend?" I asked as we were leaving the store.

"Sure, hun," Mandy answered, "what did you have in mind?"

"I don't want to say just yet. But I want to do a sort of celebration of Brad. Nothing sad or cheesy, just a fun way to remember him."

"That sounds perfect."

The two girls put their arms around me as we walked together to the car. *I can do this. I can go on living and go on loving him. It's just time that I stop being* in love *with him.*

# 14

## if i let you go

THE SUN WAS STILL LINGERING ON THE HORIZON on Saturday night when Thomas picked me up. I piled into the back seat of his SUV next to Mandy and Tess, carrying a large duffle bag in my arms.

"All right, Lil." Anna turned around from the passenger seat. "You can't keep it a secret anymore! Where are we going?"

"Just drive," I said in a low, mysterious tone. "I'll get us there."

Anna laughed as Thomas put the truck into gear.

"What in the world is in that giant bag?" Mandy asked. "I am so not dressed for camping!" She motioned to her wedge sandals and I laughed.

"You'll be fine. Seriously, do none of you know the meaning of the word *secret?*"

I navigated as Thomas took my turn-by-turn directions and we pulled into the park entrance. By the time we hit the tree line everyone had figured out where we were headed.

"I should have known you were taking us here," Anna whispered, nudging me. "It's a perfect night for it."

She was right, it was *perfect.* Just as it had been with Brad nearly five months ago. Thomas parked the SUV on the grass and we all climbed out. The group hadn't been back since school began and it had become too cool to swim in the crisp lake water. But there we were, all together. It would be perfect. *Perfect. The word carries a new definition now.*

I lead the way down towards the lake with my duffle bag bouncing off of my leg as I walked. Once again, the moon was reflecting off the water like a spotlight. I found the perfect place on the grass near the banks where the light was hitting just right. I dropped the bag, unzipped the top, and pulled out the crocheted blanket that Brad and I had used that night. Thomas grabbed the corner and with a quick jerk we sent the center billowing into the air as we slowly lowered it to the ground.

"Have a seat, guys!" I told them. I remained standing as I fished around in my duffle bag.

"She is being so mysterious tonight," Mandy exclaimed to Tess. "I like it!"

"All right, one for everyone." I passed around red plastic

cups with thin white rims and then reached back into the bag and pulled out a glass bottle. "Surprise!" I smiled, raising the bottle into the air.

"Is that champagne?" Anna squeaked. "Where did you get that?"

"I had Lizard get it for me."

"Yeah, right," Tess said with a laugh.

"No, I'm serious!" I told them.

They looked at me in astonishment.

"Since when do you talk to Lizard?" Anna asked. "Doesn't he like… hate you? And don't you hate him even more?"

"Let's just say…" I gave them a sly grin. "We have a mutual understanding."

"Who cares where she got it," Thomas chimed in. "Point is, she got it!"

He motioned for the bottle and began untwisting the wire cap as I handed it to him.

"I don't even know who you are anymore, Lillian!" Anna laughed.

"That makes two of us," I said.

There was suddenly a loud *pop*. We all jumped and watched as the cork soared through the air and landed in the lake.

"That's my man." Anna poked at Thomas's hips as he held the bottle towards us, foam bubbling from the top.

"If we had let you open it you probably would have shot me right in the face," he said, laughing while he poured the fizzy liquid into my cup.

"You know me too well," Anna told him sarcastically.

"All right," I said once everyone had champagne in their

glass. "To Brad." I raised my cup towards the center of the blanket and everyone followed suit, the plastic cups crinkled together as they touched.

"To Brad!" The group repeated as we toasted.

We all sipped in silence for a moment, until I coughed as the bubbles hit my nose unexpectedly.

"Such a rebel you're turning into, Lil," Mandy joked. "If only Brad could see you now."

My face dropped. *If only Brad could see me now…*

"Oh, I'm sorry, Lillian. I didn't mean it like that," she insisted. "I just meant…"

"No, it's okay." I let the words from Chris' book comfort me. "You're right. Brad wouldn't know what to do with me!"

Everyone laughed, and it felt good. *The pain won't go away, but sometimes you have to push it to the back.* Surprisingly, with my friends by my side, it wasn't as hard as I thought.

****

After finishing up the bottle of champagne and half a bag of cheese puffs that I produced from my duffle, we settled down and watched the ripples in the lake as the moonlight jumped from one to the other.

"Thanks for doing this with me tonight," I told everyone. "It means a lot." I looked around at their faces, they were all nodding and smiling. "I guess I really just wanted to tell you all how much it meant to me the way you instantly accepted Brad into our group of friends. I'll admit, I was afraid you would think I was crazy and freak out the first day I invited him to have lunch with us, but you didn't. You all welcomed him to our table and in no time, it was like he had always been a part of our little group. Like he belonged."

I smiled with tears in my eyes, thinking back to that December day when I nervously led Brad across the crowded cafeteria and introduced him to my friends. They knew who he was—the quiet, mysterious troublemaker who hung out with Lizard and Jones, but they still smiled and offered him a seat. Within minutes, he was joking with Thomas about the basketball game from the previous weekend and I breathed a sigh of relief.

"And I'm sorry if I acted like none of you understood how I was feeling once Brad went missing," I continued. "I guess it was just easier to throw myself a pity party and act like I was going through this all alone. But this...Brad, I mean, has affected all of us. I'm ready to stop mourning him and start celebrating him. Wherever he is."

"I must admit," Anna said. "The day you called me and told me you kissed *Brad Lee,* I *did* think you were crazy!"

Tess nudged my arm as everyone laughed.

"But then I met him," Anna continued. "I mean, really met him, not just saw him in the halls, and it was obvious what you saw in him. Brad...he's cool. Not like in the way that we all think we are." I let out a giggle. "But in a genuine 'cool' way. And he's pretty hot, no offense to you, Thomas."

"None taken."

"Knowing his reputation around school, I wasn't sure if it would last. But then he gave you this..." She reached for Brad's ring. "What was it, less than a month after you started dating?"

"Three weeks," I grinned.

"Three weeks!" she repeated. "There was no denying he was crazy about you. Anyway, there's something special about Brad. He's genuine, and fun, and always knows how to make people laugh..." Anna suddenly choked up and I watched as her eyes welled up with tears. "I am proud to be his friend."

"Me too," Mandy said with a nod, and Tess agreed.

"The first time I met Brad, he completely intimidated me. I won't lie." Thomas threw his hands into the air. "I mean, we all heard stories about his shenanigans with Lizard and Jones. I had no idea what he was capable of. And I think at one point he may have been in that group that broke into my house and stole food out of our refrigerator while my family was on vacation..."

"Yeah, that was confirmed," I said with a laugh.

Thomas nodded and a smile grew on his face. "I knew it! Anyway, despite everything I had heard about the guy, I realized within seconds of talking to him that I wanted to be his friend. He kind of oozed with a certain bro-charm, but you ladies wouldn't understand what I mean by that..."

We all laughed for a moment as we fought back tears.

"Wherever Brad is now, I just hope he knows how much we all care about him," Anna whispered.

"I'm sure he does." I nodded. "He would have loved to be here with us tonight."

We all lay on our backs, stretched across the blanket, and stared up at the stars for what felt like hours. Being there with my friends made me feel a little more whole than I had since Brad disappeared. *Maybe it really is possible for me to put myself back together.* Thomas drove us home once it got late, and I spent the night at Anna's house with the rest of the girls. We stayed up till two in the morning, watching chick flicks and giving each other manicures just like we had many times before. There were moments when it seemed like nothing had changed and I savored them. I finally felt like someone had pushed the play button on my life again.

****

I walked home from Anna's the next morning with a plan for what I would do next. My family had already left for church without me but that was okay. I needed the time to myself. There under my bed was the wooden box from Brad—the tiny coffin that contained the remaining shards of our relationship. I wanted to give it a proper burial, and I had the perfect spot.

After a long search for a hand shovel in our shed, I found the right tool and made my way into the front yard with the box. The tree outside my window appeared thicker than ever, and I wiggled in-between its branches and the side of the house. In the dark opening, I knelt down in the dirt and struck the pointed tip of the shovel into the cool ground. It barely pierced the soil, but I continued to dig until a brick-sized hole formed beneath me.

I had almost dug deep enough into the earth when I noticed something out of the corner of my eye. Near the trunk of the tree lay something light in color, covered in dirt and pine needles. I tossed the shovel aside and crawled on my knees towards it. It was a small piece of paper sticking out of the ground, with a piece of tape attached to the top of it. I touched it gingerly with two fingers and carefully retrieved it. Once in my hand, I dusted away the dirt with my fingertips, blinking ferociously in the dim light as I tried to read what it said. There was writing on it that had become wet and faded and was nearly impossible to make out. But as I read the last line of the note my heart stopped.

*I love you, Brad*

I scrambled frantically from behind the tree and held the paper up to the light. There were several lines of writing above his signature but the ink was smudged. The only other sentence I could read was at the end of the letter. It simply said, *I'm sorry*.

Clutching the note in my hand, I sprinted through the yard and towards the street, desperate to get back to Anna's house. As I ran my mind raced. *This note is from Brad from the night he disappeared. The smudge on the window....* The window. I trembled thinking of my window and how I had lied to the police about where I had last seen Brad. *If I had just told Detective Padron the truth, we may have found this months ago.*

"Anna!" I tore into the Redmond's back yard and found Anna right where she had been heading when I left, sunbathing on the back deck.

"What, do you miss me already?" she said with a laugh as she flipped over onto her back.

"Look at this!" I raced towards her with the note and shoved it into her face. "It's from him!"

She snatched it from me and brought it close to her eyes. "From who?"

"From Brad! Can you read it?"

She held it at different angles, squinting in an attempt to make out the faded words.

"I don't get it. What am I looking at here?"

"It's from Brad. From the night he disappeared. It has been under my window this whole time! It looks like he taped it to the glass but it must have fallen…"

"But, Lillian," she said, handing the note back. "What makes you think it's from that night?"

I held the paper towards her again and pointed. "Because, look. It says 'I love you'."

She looked up at me with wide eyes.

"It's from that night," I said again. "I'm sure."

Anna sat up taller. "So what do we do? Don't we need to take it to the police? Maybe they can read what it says."

"No." I shook my head. "They won't do anything. It will end up in a drawer somewhere."

"Lil, I'm just not sure what else you can do with it if you can't tell what it says." Anna shrugged her shoulders.

"I can't read it," I told her. "But I know someone who can."

"Really?" she asked excitedly. "Who?"

"I don't have time to explain. But…I…need your car."

Anna's jaw dropped as a smile grew on her face. "Wait…what is this? Is this a trick?"

"What?"

"Lillian…if you want to borrow my car just ask! You don't have to show up here with some note and claim it's from Brad…"

"No! Anna, I'm serious. Please. *Please.* I will never ask you for anything, ever again," I begged.

"Yes, you will."

"Okay…okay I probably will. But I'm begging you."

Anna stood up and placed her hands on her hips. " Good grief, Lillian. You know I'm going to say yes! Just had to make you sweat a little." She headed towards the back door. "Now hold on, I'll get you the keys."

"Thank you!" I shouted as she disappeared into the living room. "Thank you, thank you, thank you."

"Do you want me to come with you?" she asked when she returned, bedazzled key ring in hand.

"Thanks," I said. "But no. I should do this alone."

"Okay, well just be careful," Anna told me. "And I don't just mean with my car."

"I will," I promised as I threw my arms around her neck. "Thanks."

Once I had the keys in hand I took off running towards her car. The only other thing I needed before I could start my trip was waiting for me inside the drawer of my bedside table.

# 15

## remember me this way

I TORE DOWN THE HIGHWAY HEADING NORTH IN Anna's blue compact, the noon sun's rays were blinding as they penetrated the windshield. According to the GPS, my destination was just over three hours away, but I was determined to make it in two and a half. On the passenger seat beside me sat the note from under the tree, tucked safely inside Chris' book. The navigation was programmed to the address written in the front cover of the paperback, and I could only pray that I would find him at home. Chris could read the note just as he had read the waitress's scribbles that day in the diner. I knew he was my only chance to learn what the paper said and possibly put an end to the mystery of what happened to Brad.

And, in the back of my mind, I knew it might be the only way I would see Chris again. Even if only to say a proper goodbye.

I traveled for over one hundred miles, bringing me almost to the Virginia state line, until the GPS prompted me to exit onto a two-lane highway that seemed headed to nowhere. The occasional aluminum mailboxes were overgrown with vines and tall weeds and the sight of a lonely, burnt out gas station gave me the chills.

*I didn't tell Anna where I am going. I didn't tell my parents where I am going...I didn't tell anyone where am I going. I'm driving to an unknown address in the middle of nowhere in search of a guy none of my friends have even met. Am I making a huge mistake?*

My thoughts wandered and I dreamed up a small, pink handgun in Anna's glove box, which made me laugh. Anna had been terrified to hold Graham's BB gun when he set up old soda cans for target practice in our back yard. There were undoubtedly no weapons in Anna's car, with perhaps the exception of a metal nail file that had become lodged between the seats. I grabbed my cell phone from the seat beside me and glanced at the LED screen. Like a cliché in every bad horror movie Brad and I had watched together, there was no service. Even if I wanted to tell someone where I was going, I couldn't. I was in this alone.

"Turn left in three-quarters of a mile." The robotic woman's voice from the GPS made me jump and I nearly slammed my foot on the brake.

"Get a grip," I whispered aloud.

I gradually slowed the car, craning my neck to get a better look at the turn. I was being directed towards a narrow road surrounded by trees on each side. There was not another car or living soul in sight.

"Turn left," the GPS reminded me.

The car crept along at twenty miles an hour as I turned the wheel and continued onto the road, hitting bumps and potholes on the uncared-for pavement. With a glance to the navigation screen, I saw my destination was approaching on the right in half a mile. *This is it.* To my left was an unkempt plot of mobile homes, assumedly abandoned, but it was impossible to be sure. My heart was pounding as I struggled to read the numbers on the few mailboxes I passed. *What will Chris say when he sees me? Has he even realized he gave me his address when he gave me the book? Or did he give me the book so I would be able to find him?*

"Your destination is on the right."

I pressed the brake until the car was at a slow crawl and brought it to a stop. Between rows of trees was a gravel driveway, overgrown with thick weeds that sprouted up the middle. There weren't any signs forbidding my entry, so I took a deep breath and turned onto the rocky drive. In the distance, behind a grown up yard and tall shade trees, sat a little white house with a wooden porch. Potted plants and faded lawn ornaments were scattered on and around the railings.

As soon as I made it to the clearing I pulled to the side of the driveway and put Anna's car in park. I sat there for a moment, scanning the area, before turning off the engine. A rusted-out Cadillac was parked in the grass beside the house but I wasn't sure if it belonged to Chris. Thinking back to the times I had seen him around town, I realized I had never seen him in a car—he had always been on foot. I reached to the seat next to me for the book containing the note and opened the front cover to reveal the address.

*Chris Colvin*
*108611 Liberty Road*
*Gladeville, North Carolina*

I glanced up at the faded house numbers that hung on the doorframe. The navigation system had led me to the right place. I turned off the engine and slipped the keys into my front pocket. It was time. I opened the drivers' side door and closed it gently behind me, not allowing it to latch. The yard was eerily quiet, apart from the chime of a metal wind ornament that was tied to the gutter on the edge of the porch.

I walked lightly on the gravel as I headed towards the house, cringing at each crunch my tennis shoes made against the rocks. *I shouldn't be here. It doesn't feel right.* I stopped for a moment, staring at the front door and searching for any sign of movement inside the house. *But if I leave now I'll be no closer to having answers. If I leave now I may never see Brad, or Chris, again…*

I moved quickly towards the house and heard a loud creak under my feet as I stepped onto the rickety wooden porch. A weathered rocking chair sat beside the door with a blue, crocheted afghan strewn over the arm. I clenched anxious fists before raising my right hand to knock. I knocked three times, each one gradually louder, and took a step back. *Silence.* I had just begun to lift my fist again when a noise came from behind the house, like the clanking of metal. A chill ran up my spine.

Stepping slowly and quietly off the porch, I took strides around the stained, white vinyl siding walls until I had a clear view of the backyard. There in the overgrown garden was a guy in a baseball cap and dirty t-shirt, bent over as he tilled the soil. I couldn't see his face, but his broad shoulders were familiar.

"Chris?" I called out across the lawn.

He continued to work at the ground, his body moving back and forth. I took a few steps closer and spoke his name again, louder this time. "Chris?"

As I moved towards him I noticed a thin white cord running down his back. He was wearing headphones. His head was down and he didn't see me as I approached. I stretched my hand slowly towards his body, trying not to scare him, and let my fingertips graze his shoulder as I stepped closer.

"Chris?" I said with a smile.

He flinched, dropping the shovel to the ground and yanking the earbuds from his ears as he quickly straightened up. The brim of the baseball cap shaded his eyes and nose and I squinted in the sun trying to make out his facial features. As he pulled the cap from his head and lifted his chin, his eyes locked with mine. Suddenly the breath I had been attempting to catch the entire drive was sucked from my body.

"Lillian?"

I felt dizzy, my knees were weak, and I blinked rapidly as I stood there frozen, staring into his eyes. *Don't do this again. Don't imagine it's him.*

"Lillian? It's okay, it's me."

"I…" My mouth hung open and my jaw started to tremble. I reached a cautious hand towards him and let my fingertips brush his unshaven cheek as I searched his face. "Brad?"

Suddenly he threw his arms around me and pulled me into his chest. I couldn't move. My limbs hung at my sides as he squeezed, my face pressing into biceps. I tried to shake my head and tell myself to snap out of it, that I must be daydreaming again or losing my mind, but as he held me it felt familiar. My thoughts raced back to the night of graduation and the smell of his skin as he had lain with me under the stars. I wasn't dreaming. It was him. *I have found him.*

"Brad," I whispered, still clutching Chris' book in my left hand. He continued to squeeze me in a tight embrace, but something didn't seem right.

I had often dreamed up scenarios in which Brad was found, suffering from amnesia and lying in a hospital bed, or being rescued from captivity in an abandoned building, but this was neither of those. He knew who I was and he wasn't wearing shackles. This backyard reunion was a far cry from a search and rescue mission.

I pushed away from him, escaping his grasp so I could take a step back. I could feel my cheeks growing hot as I stared into his eyes. "Brad, what is going on?"

"Lillian, I've missed you so much. How did you find me?" His voice was trembling as he reached out to touch my face, but I turned away.

"I...I don't understand," I whispered. "What are you doing here?"

A gust of wind blew through the garden causing the branches and vines to sway. Loose strands of my hair whipped in front of my eyes. My head was spinning.

"I can explain everything. Please…please, Lil, give me a chance to explain."

I heard the sound of the back door opening and turned to see Chris standing in the doorway wearing the jeans and gray hoodie that I had grown to recognize.

"Chris," I said flatly, staring at him with a blank expression. His eyes were wide.

"How do you know him?" Brad asked.

"I…" I looked to Brad and then back to Chris. "How do *you* know him?"

"Chris is my brother, Lillian. There are some things I need to tell you…"

"Your *brother*?" My jaw gaped open as I searched their faces. "But he…"

"I'm so sorry," Chris mouthed.

"I need to sit down," I said, my knees trembling beneath me.

"Of course." Brad nodded. "Here…come with me. Chris, you should go inside. Check on Mom."

"Mom?" I whispered.

Brad grabbed my hand and pulled me towards an old shed behind the garden where a wooden bench acted as a lean-to for a rusty collection of garden tools. I looked over my shoulder as Chris retreated inside. I watched him disappear into the dilapidated house as Brad squeezed my hand. His touch felt rougher than I remembered. Different. Yet my fingers melted into his. I couldn't form a solid thought in my mind. *Am I dreaming? Or is this some sort of cruel trick?*

"Have a seat." He dusted a layer of dirt from off of the

bench and drew me down next to him, his fingers still laced with mine.

"What does this say?" I pulled my hand away and slipped the note out of the book. "Please tell me this note explains everything, and that you didn't just take off and leave me and everyone else…"

He took the paper from me and closed his hand around it as he dropped his head.

"It explains some things. Yes."

"Then answer me, please." I shook my head, struggling to take it all in. "Where are we? What is this place? Why are you here? And Chris…why did Chris…" I spit out the questions as quickly as they entered my mind. I looked around at the dilapidated house and the overgrown grass and then looked back to Brad who seemed right at home. Nothing was making any sense.

"Lil, I'm not sure where to start."

As he peered up at me his blue eyes were washed out from the sunlight. I was seeing him differently than I ever had before, remembering that the guy I thought I fell in love with had a rap sheet, adoption records, a lying brother and an entire past that had eluded me over the course of our relationship. As I looked at him, I wondered if the relationship I had been clinging to since May was all a lie. Was it over and I was the last to know? *Or is it ending now?*

"Brad, I don't care where you start. Please just tell me what's going on."

He ran his fingers through his hair like I had seen him do so many times before. Somehow, it still made my heart jump.

"This house belongs to my uncle," he started slowly. "He's my mom's brother, my biological mom that is. I know I never told you I was adopted, or that I had a brother, and I'm so sorry..."

"I already know that you were adopted, Brad. Montana told me...in one way or another." I let out a heavy sigh. "There are a lot of things you didn't tell me that I had to find out from other people. Or from the *police*..." I had to stop myself. "Go on."

His eyes widened. "Mom is sick, Lil. Like, really sick. She was looking for me, and when my uncle found my graduation announcement online he tracked me down."

*The man who came to Lizard's.*

"That night, after I took you home, he stopped me on the road and said he wanted me to come with him to see my mom." He finished his sentence with an emphasis as if he was done. The end.

I shook my head. "And then what? You jumped in his car and never looked back? Brad, this doesn't make any sense!"

"No! I never intended to just up and *leave* the way I did...it was never meant to be for more than a day or two."

"Well what happened? Why did you stay?"

"I...I panicked. I just got so overwhelmed. Seeing her, talking with her, getting to know her again...I didn't know how I could leave her. My mom isn't the same person she was when I was a kid." His tone of voice changed suddenly. More desperate. "Mom's liver is failing, Lil. She's dying."

"Brad, I'm sorry...but I still don't understand..."

"She wanted to find me because she needed me to forgive

her for giving me up. She wanted to make sure she found me before it was too late. And deep down, I knew I needed to see her to forgive her, too. Despite everything that happened, everything she put me through, I still love her."

His words sounded as though they could have come out of my own mouth. *Despite everything, everything he put me through, I have continued loving him. But is love enough?*

"But what about your family?" I asked, dropping my head. "Why couldn't you just pick up the phone and explain to them what was happening…"

"I wanted to tell my parents," he said. "But what would they think? They had lined up a perfect future for me, with a good job, and I was supposed to start college in the fall with the money they had saved up for me for so long. I know it sounds like excuses…but I wasn't sure how to tell them that I was willing to give all of that up to be with the woman who abandoned me when I was ten years old."

"And what is your excuse for not telling *me?*" I wanted an answer, but I couldn't think of a single excuse that would make it okay.

"I tried to." Brad opened his hand, revealing the weathered note. "I taped this to your window, I thought you would see it the next morning."

"But what does it say? Does it explain everything you just told me?"

"It says, *I have to go away for a little while. I'm sorry, but please don't worry. I hope you know how much I love you.*" He sighed as he handed it back to me.

Another lump was forming in my throat. "Five months

isn't a little while, Brad. It's a long, long time…"

"I know. I'm so sorry. I didn't think this through, it all just kind of happened." He put his hands on my shoulders and tried to pull me close to him. "I couldn't tell you where I was going without telling you *everything*. I mean, it's like I had this whole different life that I had never told you about and suddenly it was too late to come clean…"

"So why not just tell me the truth?" I asked, the words barely screeching out. His eyes drifted to the ground. "Brad?"

"I was afraid," he finally said. "I was afraid of what would happen if you knew the truth about me. I was afraid you wouldn't want to be with me if…"

"I was afraid, too!" I cried. "Afraid you were kidnapped or *dead*."

"I know." His head was shaking. "Lillian, please…. Everything is going to be okay."

A flood of emotions rushed through me and tears suddenly began to stream uncontrollably down my cheeks. I threw my hands into the air, jerking away from his grasp as I rose to my feet.

"Nothing is okay!" I shouted. "*I'm* not okay! I haven't been okay since the morning I found out you were gone. No, not gone," I corrected myself. "*Missing*. They found a body that was checked against your dental records, Brad. They pulled DNA off your *toothbrush!*"

"I had no idea…"

"What did you think was happening, Brad? Did you think everyone just accepted the fact that you were gone and moved on? Did you think no one cared that you were missing? Our entire community has been looking for you!"

He dropped his face into his hands.

"I spent the last five months searching for your corpse in ditches and dumpsters, attending prayer vigils, questioning everything I believe in and practically yelling at God because I didn't understand how He could have let this happen. I lay awake night after night because I couldn't bear to dream about you...all because you didn't just tell me the truth..."

When he looked up at me, I could see tears forming in his eyes. "I'm sorry—so sorry. I don't know what else to say, you just have to believe me," he pleaded.

"Why should I believe you now, Brad?" I cried. "You're acting like walking away from your life is a perfectly normal, excusable thing. How can I believe anything you say when you've done this and kept so many things from me?"

He wiped his face with the palm of his hand. "I don't know. I'm just begging you to try..."

"What about Chris? Did you send your own brother to join in on the search party for you?"

"What?" he asked. "No, of course not."

"Did you know that he was befriending me and acting like he understood what I was going through?"

He shook his head, standing. "No, Lillian. I swear."

"And when you came back to tell me you loved me that night..." I whispered. "Was that your cowardly way of telling me goodbye?"

"Of course not, Lil," Brad insisted, reaching for me. "Everything I said that night was true. I came to your window before I ever knew that my uncle was in town. I promise you, it had *nothing* to do with my leaving. And I love you just as much now as I did then…"

I struggled to catch my breath, feeling as though I had used up the last of my strength. "How did this happen? How could you let this happen? How did we get here…" My legs were trembling underneath me as I let my body collapse into his chest. He wrapped his arms tightly around me.

"I am so, so sorry," he whispered as he held me. "I'll never be able to tell you how sorry I am."

"It wouldn't have mattered," I whimpered, sobbing into his shirt. "I didn't care who you were before me. All I cared about was who you were when we were together."

Our arms remained intertwined for a long moment. Once my crying subsided, I raised my head and looked into his eyes. He lowered his lips towards mine and before I could pull away we were locked in a deep, time-stopping kiss. My heart was racing and suddenly we were back on my living room floor, sitting in front of the fireplace, embracing each other for the first time. *If only it were possible to go back to that day and start all over again. Forget all of this.* But as my eyes opened, we were back in the yard, hours from home.

"Just come with me, Brad," I said as I motioned towards Anna's car. "You have to come back and tell everyone you're okay."

This time, he was the first to pull away. His hands swept down my arms and caught the tips of my fingers. "I can't, Lil."

"What?" I took a step back. "What do you mean, you can't?"

"I can't leave my mom. Not now. She…she doesn't have

much time left." His voice broke. "I know this must sound crazy to you, but you can come visit me anytime, we can still be together…"

"This isn't only about *me*, Brad. Your family, the one that raised you, needs to see you too."

I searched his face, trying to read his thoughts, but his expression had gone blank.

"Wait…" I swallowed. "Are you asking me to pretend like you're still missing? Is that what you're asking me to do? Haven't you let this go on long enough?"

He barely nodded but his eyes blinked as a response. And just like that, without so much as another word, I knew it was over. *It has to be over.*

"I need to go." I reached into my pocket for Anna's keys and started to back away from him.

"What?" He extended his hand towards me. "No, don't go. My mom is inside. I want you to meet her."

"No."

"Lillian, please. I love you. I've loved you this entire time…"

"Stop! Stop saying you love me after everything you have put me through. I can't lie to our friends and family and act like I don't know where you are! And if you really loved me you wouldn't be asking me to do this."

"Whatever you need to do Lil, do it, but please don't leave like this. You don't understand. I can't leave her now."

He moved in towards me and placed his hand on my waist. Feeling his touch on my hip I held my breath, tempted to fall into his arms again, but memories of the past five months were stronger than the moment. No matter how hard it would be to let go of him, it was my only choice. *Choices. For once, I get to make the choices.*

"I have been defending you to the police, my parents, our friends, practically the entire town, from the very first day you disappeared. I swore to myself and to everyone else that you would *never* have just left us, even after I learned the truth about your past. And I was willing to look like a fool for *not knowing* so many things about you because I loved you despite all of that…"

"But, Lil, I love you too. I never stopped…"

"Wait." I put my hand out. "I'm not finished. How can I keep loving you when I feel like I don't even know you anymore? The truth is that everyone else was right about you. You chose to leave. You chose to leave me."

"It isn't like that, Lillian. Please, you know it's not…"

"I can't lie to your family and our friends and pretend like you're still gone, Brad. You have put them through enough. You've put *me* through enough. They deserve the truth just like I do. And if you aren't going to be the one to tell them, I will."

He was frozen with his jaw clenched and eyelids heavy. For a moment perhaps he understood what it was like to have his entire world crashing in on him.

"Just give me some time to think about this," he begged. "Please."

"What is there to think about?"

"My mom abandoned me. I can't do the same thing to her."

"And what do you think you did to me?" I whispered.

His lips parted as though he were going to speak, but no words left his mouth. I hunted his eyes for any sign of compassion. They were blank, almost cold. I had lost him.

I slowly slipped the chain that held his class ring over my head and placed it in his hand. "Goodbye, Brad."

"Don't do this," he cried. "Lillian, wait."

I pulled the keys from my pocket and squeezed the sharp metal edges into my fist as I turned to walk to the car. I needed to feel the pain to keep me from breaking down. I heard a few soft footsteps behind me, but they stopped. He wasn't coming after me. I moved as quickly as I could without breaking into a full-blown sprint, slowing only when my fingers reached the cool metal of the door handle.

"Lillian!" Brad called out one last time. "Please, Lil."

I didn't look up until I was seated behind the steering wheel, fumbling with the key ring in my trembling hands as I tried to start the ignition. Brad stood on the front porch of the old house, and behind him the door opened and a woman stepped outside. She was tall and thin with hollow cheeks, dressed in a long nightgown. The engine let out a low *hum* as I placed my hand on the gearshift, but I waited a moment longer before I put the car into reverse.

This frail, sick woman standing just a few hundred feet away from me was the root cause of five months of heartache for myself and everyone else who loved Brad. I wanted to hate her, for what she did to Brad as a child and what she was doing now. But as she clutched Brad's arm and struggled to keep herself upright, it was clear she wasn't a villain. She was just as broken as the rest of us.

I raised one hand towards them to wave goodbye. Brad dropped his head towards his mom in response. *I can't be angry with him for choosing her.*

"I forgive you," I whispered to myself.

I felt myself smiling through my tears as I drove along the highway in Anna's little blue car and I wasn't sure why. Leaving Brad, watching him reeling in the rearview mirror when I pulled away, was nothing to smile about. Yet I suddenly felt lighter, refreshed even, as I made my way back to town. The sun was setting behind me as though the beautiful burning rays were leading me home. *Maybe I am smiling because it's over. Well, almost. It's over and I made it. I survived.*

My phone lay on the seat beside me and I knew I should call the Lees and tell them what I had found, but I hadn't found the words to say yet. They needed to know Brad was okay, but I wondered if knowing that he chose to abandon them would provide any actual closure. Seeing him, touching him, and looking into his eyes when I told him goodbye was enough for me. They would probably need the same. They, too, would need to know it was over and they had made it.

# 16

## sometimes goodbye is a second chance

I DROVE ANNA'S CAR DIRECTLY TO THE LEE'S house, but by the time I arrived they already knew what I was going to say. Brad had called them and relayed the same story he had told me. Montana rushed down the stairs to the foyer and threw her arms around my waist when she saw me.

"You found him! You found him, Lillian!" she shrieked with excitement. "I can't believe you did."

I looked up at Janice as she wiped a tear from her cheek. "She sure did, honey."

We weren't all sharing Montana's childlike enthusiasm.

"Thank you for all that you have done, Lillian." Mr. Lee hugged me and then squeezed my shoulders as he looked me in the eye. "You really stuck with us through this whole ordeal."

*So, now it's an ordeal.* "Honestly, I didn't know what else to do, sir."

"Please, call me Mark."

I nodded and offered him a small smile before exchanging goodbyes with the entire Lee family, minus one prodigal son. As I walked down the front steps towards his muddy truck that was still parked in the driveway, I realized Brad was no longer a *first-name last-name guy.* He was, once again, Brad Colvin. I had to admit it had a certain ring to it.

I headed to Anna's and returned her car, offering an abridged version of the day's events that concluded with, 'I found him, he's fine, but please don't ask me any more questions right now.' Being the best friend she was, she cried as she hugged me and told me to call her when I was ready to talk. I wasn't sure what I was ready for, but I wasn't ready to talk. I was ready to go home, crawl in bed, and forget the last five months ever happened.

I handed her the keys to her car and decided to walk the rest of the way home, insisting I needed the air. As I took in the crisp, fall breeze, marveling at the leaves that had turned bright shades of orange and red, I rehearsed the speech I would give my parents. *It was for the best. He did it for his family. I made the right decision to leave him there. I'm not going to regret walking away from the love of my life. It was easy to leave him there....* I started to wonder who I was actually trying to convince—my family or myself. *Will I regret walking away from him? Or could I ever have continued a relationship with him after everything he put me through?*

Once I neared my yard I looked down the road and noticed a familiar car in my driveway. It was the same brown, rusty Cadillac I had seen parked at the house in Gladeville. *Brad. He came back for me.* Oddly enough, the car was parked in the exact spot where I remembered seeing Detective Padron's squad car on the first night after Brad disappeared. I ran across the grass and the driver's side door opened as I approached.

"Lillian," Chris said as he gently closed the car door behind him. "Hi."

"Hi." I stopped a few feet away from him. "What are you doing here?"

"I owe you an explanation."

"No." I shook my head. "You don't owe me anything."

"I wanted to tell you the truth. I even tried…I just didn't know how to say it. And, honestly, I didn't think I could stand to see your face when you found out the truth." He took a few steps towards me, fidgeting with the sleeves of his gray hoodie. "I couldn't be the one to hurt you like that."

"I understand."

"I really did understand what you were going through," he said. "When we were kids and Mom couldn't take care of us, she sent me to live with my uncle. But he didn't have room for Brad, and before I knew it Mom had given him up and he was gone. I spent the last eight years wondering what happened to my brother, never knowing if he was safe or even alive. I hadn't seen him until the night Uncle Jack showed up with him at our house…"

"The night of graduation."

He nodded. "Mom got out of jail three years ago and decided she was ready to be sober. We've been looking for him ever since."

"But how did you know about me?" I asked.

"Are you kidding?" He smiled. "Brad couldn't stop talking about you, telling Mom all about how incredible you were and how you were the best thing that had ever happened to him. I felt like I had to meet you. Based on his description of you, I couldn't figure out how he was able to leave you behind."

I dropped my head and my eyes explored the tiny cracks in the pavement. "So, once you met me, did you figure it out?" I asked softly.

"No. I still can't." He stared off across the yard for a moment before looking back at me. "Look, Lil, I know what I said about Brad that day at the lake. About how you didn't deserve what he was doing to you…"

I shook my head. "Chris…"

"And I still think that's true," he continued. "You don't deserve that. But, I saw how he looked after you left today. I hope you realize how much he cares about you, even if he hasn't done a good job of showing it. Everything that has gone on with our mom put him in a really tough spot. He didn't mean for things to happen the way they did."

"I know."

"And…I didn't either."

I turned up one corner of my mouth. "I don't blame you for anything, Chris. Really. Honestly, I probably wouldn't have believed you if you *had* told me the truth. And anyway, I should thank you."

"Thank me? For what?"

"The book."

Chris dropped his head and nodded. "Right. The book."

"See, really, you *did* tell me about Brad. In one way or another. It just took me awhile to realize it." I cocked my head to look into his tired eyes. They were partially hidden behind strands of his hair as Brad's often were. "Does he know you are here?"

"No way," he said. "He probably thinks I took off to avoid him kicking my butt once he found out I had been sneaking down here to see you. Which is the other reason that I left." He smirked and I couldn't help but let out a chuckle.

"Are you going to be okay?" I asked after a moment.

"Yeah, of course. Don't worry about me." He took another step towards me. "Are *you* going to be okay?"

"Yes." I cracked a small grin. "After I re-define the meaning of 'okay'."

We exchanged goodbyes and shared a long hug before I watched him back the old car slowly towards the street. My parents were standing in the living room window watching as I waved to him. They had a lot of questions. I only had a few answers.

"Things are going to be different around here, I promise," I whispered as I hugged my dad and then my mom.

After chatting briefly with Lizard, I turned off my cell phone to silence the constant alerts as I received endless texts and phone calls asking about Brad. I wasn't sure how the word had gotten out, but I suspected Montana and Anna both had a hand in spreading the news. Mom baked my favorite homemade macaroni and cheese for dinner that night and I gorged on the creamy, custard-colored noodles until the button on my jeans was ready to pop. Graham and Eliza insisted I join them in a game after dinner, and I laughed with them as we sat on the floor around the coffee table.

I was desperately trying to feel 'normal', yet I felt like I was having an out-of-body experience, watching myself joking and smiling even though I wasn't actually experiencing the emotions. Despite the colorful, fast-moving card game, my mind kept racing back to the image of Brad and his mom on the porch. I lost for the second time, then hugged each member of my family and retreated to my room. I needed to be alone with my thoughts.

Behind my closed bedroom door, I sat on my bed with my legs dangling off the edge, letting my toes brush back and forth against the plush strands of the rug. I stared blankly at the photos taped around the vanity mirror as my eyes went in and out of focus. Brad was there, smiling back at me, as always, but his smile looked different than I had remembered. I could see now that even in the pictures with me there was a touch of sadness in his eyes. *Maybe now he will find what he has been looking for.*

Below the collage of photos, a handful of college pamphlets were stacked neatly where my mom had left them in May. *Maybe I am finally ready to get away from here. Maybe I can go to college and find what I have been looking for. Maybe I can learn how to help kids like Brad, and Chris. Maybe the past five months haven't been completely in vain. Just maybe.*

I collapsed backward onto my bed, legs still hanging off the edge, and realized there was one thing I hadn't done since finding Brad. I hadn't prayed. But this time, I didn't want to pray a whiny prayer, begging for this and that and questioning why things were happening to me. I wanted to express my thankfulness. As hard as it was to grasp, I was still thankful that I knew the truth. I squinted my eyes shut, biting my lower lip as I attempted to silently form a sentence, but the words didn't come. I wasn't sure how to pray it. Not yet.

Pulling open the small drawer in the top of my nightstand, I rummaged through old birthday cards and tubes of lip balm until I found the small, blank journal I had received as a gift from my aunt on my sixteenth birthday and a purple gel pen. *If I can't think of the words, maybe I can write them.* I sat up and rested the small of my back against my pillow before bringing my knees towards me and placing the open book against them. I pressed the tip of the pen to the paper and began to write.

*Dear Brad,*

It was far from a prayer, but suddenly words were rushing through my hand and appearing in the ink on the page.

*I thought your disappearance had broken me. But now I realize that you were broken long before I was. While I saw you as my rock, you were the one who was crumbling beneath me. It hurts me that I didn't see it. But I think what hurts me more than anything is that you didn't want me to know the truth about your past. There is nothing you could have told me about yourself that would have made me love you less. Knowing the truth would have only made me love the person you have become even more. I naïvely thought that who we were before we were together didn't matter, but I was wrong. I lost part of myself while I was looking for you, and now I have to re-discover who I was before you, to figure out who I am without you.*

I dropped the pen into the crease between the pages and started to close the book but something stopped me. There was one thing left to say.

*I'll always remember you, and I'll always love you. Even if you're gone.*

# acknowledgments

There are so many people to acknowledge, but first and foremost I must thank God for the many blessings in my life. I strive to use my gifts for His glory.

*If You're Gone* grew out of a novella I wrote in eighth grade and I am so grateful to my parents for always supporting my creative endeavors and making me feel like I could accomplish anything. Fast-forward a decade to when I met my incredible husband, John, who has encouraged me and gone along with every project I've ever dreamed up. Thank you, John, for believing in me even when I didn't believe in myself.

I'm just going to continue with the Thank You's because there aren't many more words I can come up with at the moment that express my gratefulness! Thank you to Stephanie for reading that dreadful first draft and providing some much needed harsh feedback while giving me insight into the world of publishing. And to Morgan, for your suggestions and support. You have been a ray of sunshine in my inbox despite the fact that we have never met. To Justin, one of the most talented people I have ever met who always makes time to answer my call, I am so grateful for your friendship and encouragement.

I must also acknowledge two selfless women who keep up invaluable websites devoted to the missing. Jerrie Dean, founder of Missing Persons of America, and Meaghan Good, founder of The Charley Project—thank you for your hard work and dedication to your cause. Your efforts don't go unnoticed.

And I can't say enough about the group who brought my characters to life in the *If You're Gone* trailer. Tara, Adam, Valkyrie, Elise, John, Shayna, James and Wade, thank you for offering your talents to the project. And to Emory and the fabulous group of extras who braved the wind and cold, it wouldn't have been the same without you!

I'd have a whole separate book if I named everyone who has inspired and supported me over the years, so I will express a wide-spread thanks to all of my family, friends and fans who pre-ordered, pre-read, shared, encouraged, praised, and constructively critiqued. I have been blessed with an incredible support network for which I am extremely thankful.

## about the author

Brittany Goodwin is an author, performer, screenwriter and director, best known for the internationally distributed faith-based feature films, *Secrets in the Snow* and *Secrets in the Fall*, which have both been awarded the highest honor of five Doves from the Dove Foundation.

Brittany lives outside Nashville, TN with her husband and every growing number of rescue pets. She enjoys traveling with her hubby and dogs, DIY projects, quoting John Hughes films, playing (and winning!) movie trivia games, and binge-watching Investigation Discovery Channel. A self-proclaimed armchair detective, Brittany is an active member of many Missing Persons blogs and Facebook pages, which inspired the topic of her debut novel, *If You're Gone*.

www.brittanygoodwin.com
Twitter: @thewritebritt

P.S. In filmmaking there are always deleted scenes, and although it is a novel, *If You're Gone* has a deleted "scene" of it's own! Curious what Lillian is up to eight years later? Does she ever reconnect with Brad? You can read the epilogue that didn't quite make the "final cut" exclusively on my website!

www.brittanygoodwin.com/ifyouregone

Thanks for reading!

Much love,

Brittany

CPSIA information can be obtained
at www.ICGtesting.com
Printed in the USA
LVHW05s2036171018
593922LV00010BA/775/P